HIRO

REAPER-Patriots

Book TWENTY-FOUR

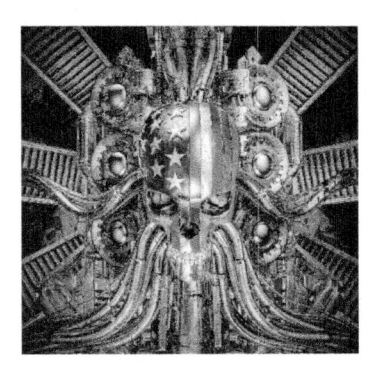

Mary Kennedy

INSATIABLE INK

Copyright © 2022 by Mary Kennedy

All rights reserved.

This book is a work of fiction. The names, characters, places, and incidents are products of the writer's imagination or have been used fictitiously and are not to be constructed as real. Any resemblance to persons, living or dead, actual events, locales, or organizations is entirely coincidental.

No part of this book may be reproduced in any form or by any electronic or mechanical means, including information storage and retrieval systems, without written permission from the author, except for the use of brief quotations in a book review.

Editing provided by: pccProofreading

MAP of Belle Fleur and Cottage Assignments

Readers – if you're like me – you're very visual – I hope this map helps as you're reading.

Readers – you'll notice some changes on the map to make it clearer and easier to read. The characters have the same cottage numbers, it just looks different. I've also added a guide to the families and books at the back. I hope you find these resources helpful.

G1-8 = Garçonnière
Big House = Belle Fleur – main house of Matthew and Irene Robicheaux, with George & Mary
The Grove – where BBQ's, picnics, and family gatherings take place

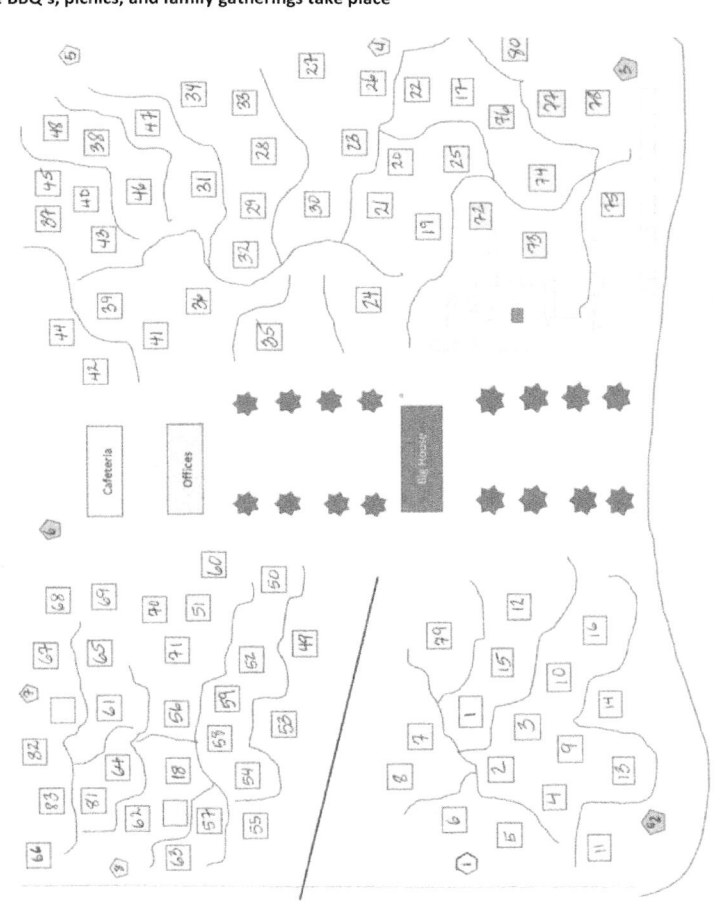

COTTAGE Assignments

1	Miller & Kari	31	Hawk & Keegan	61	Hunter & Megan	83	
2	Alec & Lissa	32	Eagle & Tinley	62	Cam & Kate	84	
3	Gabe & Tori	33	Ace & Charlie	63	Jax & Ellie	85	
4	Gaspar & Alex	34	Razor & Bella	64	Adam & Jane	86	
5	Raphael & Savannah	35	Tango & Taylor	65	Ben & Harper	87	
6	Baptiste & Rose	36	Gunner & Darby	66	Carl & Georgie	88	
7	Antoine & Ella	37	Ghost & Grace	67	Striker & Violet	88	
8	Ivan & Sophia	38	Zulu & Gabi	68	Molly & Asia	89	
9	Tristan & Emma	39	Doc & Bree	G1	Hiro	90	
10	Luc & Montana	40	Paul & Elizabeth	G2	Winter	91	
11	King & Claire	41	Luke & Ajei	G3	Aiden & Brit	92	
12	Sly & Suzette	42	Fitz & Zoe	G4	Eric & Sophia Ann	93	
13	Rory & Piper	43	RJ & Celia	69	Kiel & Liz	94	
14	O'Hara & Lucia	44	Carter & Ani	70	Joseph & Julia	95	
15	Titus & Olivia	45	Bull & Lily	71	Wes & Virginia	96	
16	Max & Riley	46	Trev & Ashley	72	Dalton & Calla	97	
17	Stone & Bronwyn	47	Whiskey & Kat	73	Nathan & Katrina	98	
18	Jazz & Gray	48	Tailor & Lena	74	Keith & Susie	99	
19	Vince & Ally	49	Angel & Mary	75	Marc & Ela	100	
20	Phoenix & Raven	50	Bryce & Ivy	76	Jake & Claudette	101	
21	Noah & Tru	51	Wilson & Sara	77	Frank & Lane	102	
22	Griff & Amanda	52	Mac & Rachelle	78	Ian & Aspen	103	
23	Gibbie & Dhara	53	Nine & Erin	79	Doug & Miguel	104	
24	Blade & Suzette	54	Clay & Adele	80	Dom	105	
25	Skull	55	Trak & Lauren	G5	Parker & Dani	106	
26	Axel & Cait	56	Lars & Jessica	G6	Michael	107	
27	Sniff & Lucy	57	Ian & Faith	G7	Sean & Shay	108	
28	Noa & Kelsey	58	Zeke & Noelle	G8	Ryan & Paige	109	
29	Eli & Jane	59	Jean & Ro	81		110	
30	Grant & Evie	60	Dexter & Marie	82			

CHAPTER ONE

Hirohito Tanaka looked over at his tiny, six-year-old hand linked with that of his grandfather's. The wrinkled skin sagged over his knuckles like a sweater that was too loose for his body. His steps were slow and sure, without making any sound at all. He tried to copy his grandfather's movements, the way his feet touched the earth, but seemingly floated.

They made this walk every Sunday while his parents attempted to fit in at the Christian church they'd chosen in their neighborhood. So far, they weren't forcing Hiro to join them, but he suspected that his grandfather had a great deal to do with that.

Hiro's father was determined that they would fit in as true Americans, doing all things in the American way. He even requested that his wife not cook as many dishes with rice. There would be no temples or karate lessons for his son, only baseball and Christianity. Yoriko Tanaka did not agree with his son. He wanted his grandson to understand where he'd come from and to be proud of his heritage, embracing all that his culture had to offer and then making the right decisions for his own life as an adult.

Hiro looked up at his grandfather once more, smiling at his hero. Their walk to the park was the favorite part of his week. Sometimes they wouldn't say anything to one another, just walk. Sometimes they would talk for hours about everything and anything.

"Are we going to participate today, Grandfather?" he asked.

The slow-motion movements of martial arts fascinated Hiro, and he loved when his grandfather allowed him to take part. Most days, he would just sit and watch, abiding by his son and daughter-in-law's wishes to keep Hiro away from their culture. Today would not be one of those days.

"Yes, Hirohito, we will participate today. Remember to listen to the teacher and move slowly, with thought and purpose. You must practice patience in the way that you move. It will serve you well one day and, most likely, will save your life or the life of another."

"I promise, Grandfather."

Yoriko gripped Hiro's small shoulders and lined him up next to him, pointing him in the direction of the other, mostly elderly, students. Hiro was so excited, he worried he might embarrass himself. His little face had a serious expression as he watched his grandfather staring straight ahead, methodically moving with the other students.

The young boy watched, repeating each movement. He took note of the angle of his hands, the placement of his feet, the delicate way that he pressed into the earth. It was difficult and beautiful all at the same time. His little legs were beginning to feel tired and shaky, then as suddenly as it had begun, it was over.

When they were done, his grandfather reached inside his bag and handed him a bag of donut holes and a small milk. He ruffled the boy's hair, smiling at him.

"That was amazing, Grandfather!"

"You were very good, Hirohito. You are a natural."

"Will I be able to come back? I mean, I know Mom and Dad don't want me to, but I don't know why."

"They are ashamed of where they have come from," frowned the old man. "Listen to me, Hirohito. When I was a younger man, I did some things that I was not very proud of. Things that put my family in danger."

"Were you a spy?" he asked enthusiastically. The old man smiled down at the boy.

"No, I was not a spy, but I did help my country's enemies. You see, Hirohito, my Emperor was a man filled with visions of ruling the world. He didn't care how he did it, or who died, even his own people. He put a plan in place to drop bombs on the United States."

Hiro's eyes grew wide, listening more intently.

"He sent young men, many only ten or twelve years older than you are now, to drop bombs on the sitting American ships. They were not even in open water able to defend themselves. It was cowardly and foolish. When they ran out of bombs, they flew their planes into the ships, killing hundreds of men.

"We heard the news in Japan, and we knew that our Emperor would be sending us to war. I was a pilot that had not participated in the attacks. They thought I was too valuable to conduct a suicide mission."

"Like the men that crashed into the ships?" asked Hiro.

"Yes, my sweet grandson, like those men, some of whom were my friends. I became quite famous for my abilities, and eventually, I knew that the Americans would win the war. I no longer believed in my Emperor and what he wanted. I wanted peace. I wanted to help and to give support to a country I believed in."

"Were you a spy, Grandpa?" The old man looked off in the distance, an expression of pain and loss filling his old features.

"I was not a spy, but it was the same. I told the Americans what my country was doing and where they would be. I was a traitor, and I paid dearly for it."

"Did you have to give them money, Grandfather?" asked the boy.

"No, Hirohito, I gave them my wife and my child. Then, I came here and married your grandmother. We had one son. Your father." He was quiet for several minutes and then pulled his grandson closer to his body. "You are a warrior, Hirohito. It is in your blood to fight for others and defend what is right. I know that your parents do not wish for you to learn our ways, but I am going to teach you without their permission. There are men, men who believe that I should be punished for what I did. One day they will come. It will be too late for me, but not for you.

"You must grow to be a strong warrior, Hirohito. Fight for those that cannot fight for themselves. Be patient and kind until it is no longer a viable option. Protect the innocent and kill those that wish to harm others. They will come, Hirohito, but you must live on so that you can save the woman that you will one day love."

"I only love you and mother and father," he said, staring at the old man. He grinned, wiping the donut glaze from the boy's face.

"And I love you," he whispered. "Come, we will visit with Master Yu and discuss your training."

For Hiro, it was the start of the most amazing part of his childhood. Every Sunday, he and his grandfather would go to the park and then to the karate studio. He discovered that he was an apt student, capable of learning quickly and demonstrating the skills immediately. Although his parents knew about their Sunday trips, they never spoke of it in front of his grandfather.

On the day of his twelfth birthday, their family celebrated with a cake and a few of his friends, his grandfather sitting quietly off to the side. Earlier in the day, he'd given Hiro a birthday card with the best gift he could ever ask for inside. Since then, he'd been quiet all day, and it worried Hiro that perhaps he wasn't feeling well.

"Are you well, Grandfather?"

"There is a storm coming, Hirohito. You need to be prepared." Hiro looked out the windows of his family's home and frowned. There wasn't a cloud in the sky. Nodding at his grandfather, he went off to play with his friends. After the party ended, the mess cleaned from their day of celebration, Hiro lay in his bed wondering what it would be like to be a teenager next year. He heard the soft knock on their front door and walked into the hallway.

"Stay here," said his grandfather quietly. "Don't wake your parents." He nodded, walking back into his bedroom. He could hear the voices below speaking Japanese.

"It is time, Yoriko Tanaka," said a man.

"Not here," said his grandfather, "in the backyard, away from my family."

Hiro debated on whether or not to wake his father, but instead, carefully made his way downstairs and toward the big windows looking out at his grandfather's precious Japanese gardens. He was kneeling on the small wooden bridge they'd built together over the pond, two men with swords standing beside him.

"You have been found guilty of treason to your Emperor," said the man.

"He is not my Emperor. The Emperor I knew is long dead. I am an old man, and this is my time."

They were his last words as the man raised the sword, swinging it artfully across his grandfather's neck. Hiro wanted to scream, wanted to yell at the men to get away, but he knew that if he did, he would die as well. He ran upstairs to wake his parents, but when he arrived in their bedroom, they were both seated on the edge of their bed, looking out the window. His father turned to stare at him, a lone tear in his eye.

"Go to bed, Hiro," said his father.

"But..."

"Bed, Hiro. Now."

Hiro never knew what happened to his grandfather's body. In the morning, it was as if he'd never existed. The blood was washed away, the body gone, his things neatly packed and stored in the attic, and his parents acted as though nothing had occurred. When friends asked about him, they would simply say that he'd returned to Japan to die alone. They all knew it was a lie, but his parents insisted on continuing the ruse.

"Father? Who were those men?" he asked.

"Hiro, you must never speak of those men again. Never. Get ready for school. You won't be attending your martial arts classes any longer." Hiro had never defied his father in his whole life. Never. His grandfather's gift would give him the chance to continue what they'd started together.

"Yes, I will. I'm sorry, Father, I don't mean to be disrespectful, but this was important to me and to Grandfather. I'm very good at it, and I will continue with my lessons. He told me that he paid for them until I turned eighteen. It was his gift to me for my birthday. I'm going to respect grandfather and go."

"You are a fool, just like your grandfather. You will never fit into this country if you continue to play into their stereotypes." Hiro was only twelve, but he understood.

"I already fit in, Father. You don't see, but I do. I practice martial arts, but I also play baseball. I fit in just fine." Hiro knew that his father and he were both miracle babies. When his grandfather married his second wife, he was already in his fifties. When Hiro was born, his father was also in his fifties, his mother in her early forties. He was a miracle child. A disappointing miracle child.

It wouldn't be the only time that Hiro defied his father. He went against him on many other occasions, including his decision to join the Army after high school. His grades were in the top five percent of his class, so college seemed inevitable, but Hiro had other ideas. His grandfather had instilled in him the desire to give back to a country that had given them so much. Although Hiro was American by birth, he never took for granted how fortunate he was. The desire to protect and serve seemed deep-rooted, despite his father's anger.

"You're throwing your life away!" he yelled.

"Father, you and I both know that's not true. I will continue my education while in the military and still serve my country." He waited a heartbeat, watching his father's anger rise. "I will serve my country just as my grandfather did. You thought I wouldn't know, that I didn't ask, but I did. Grandfather taught me much, even though you wouldn't listen to him. I'm proud of what he did for our country."

Hiro didn't speak much to his family once he left for boot camp. His mother wrote an occasional letter, but his father's stubborn streak was hard to break through. He suffered a stroke while Hiro was deployed, succumbing shortly thereafter. It wasn't long after that, and his mother began showing the first signs of dementia. Now, she didn't even recognize herself, let alone her son.

Fulfilling his promise to his parents, and more importantly to himself and to his grandfather, he received his master's degree, but he did it his way. He served his nation first, and then got his education.

Hiro's main goal was to become an Army Ranger, but every time he attempted to apply, his commanding officer would tell him it wasn't the right time. He'd learned many things from his grandfather; patience was the biggest. All things would come in time and wherever you were, is where you were supposed to be. Hiro lived those words every day of his life.

What no one knew, not even his parents, was that Hiro had remembered every face of every man responsible for his grandfather's death. Their images were imprinted on his brain, and he made sure that when it was time, he hunted them down and killed them all, one by one.

He never dreamed that his chance encounter with Devin Parker would lead him to his ultimate dream and his ultimate team. In between jobs after leaving the security agency he was working for, he'd reached out to Parker to see what he was up to. Devin was a big man, tall and muscular, but he was an even better Ranger and always fought for Hiro to enter. He was shocked to get a call back with an offer to help the ultimate security team.

"Parker, brother, it's nice to see you," he said with a big, beautiful smile. Hiro was a solid six-feet of lean, yet full muscles. He moved like a cat, graceful and deadly all at the same time. The brownstone near D.C. was in a quiet, upscale neighborhood.

"Hirohito Tanaka, you're a sight for sore eyes, brother," said Parker, pulling him in for a man-hug.

"I was surprised to get your call," he said, smiling at Parker. Hiro glanced around the room of men standing against the walls. Their bearing told him they were all Special Forces, and most likely, the very best the world had to offer. It didn't escape Hiro that they were also extremely tall and large. Staring at the room, he nodded at Parker. "I'm glad to see you doing well."

"I am, thanks, brother. Hiro, these are the men and woman from REAPER-Patriots, the group I told you about."

"You didn't need to tell me much," he smiled. "I know all about you. I worked for Gravity Security for a few years after I left the Army. They weren't really my cup of tea, but when Parker called, I was intrigued. He says you need someone to get on the inside of Dallas Stevens' organization."

It was the beginning of a new life for Hirohito Tanaka. Offered a role within the organization, he jumped at the opportunity. The men and women of RP were exactly the kind of people he wanted to be associated with, and Mama Irene was exactly the influence he needed in his life.

The first day of training, he was tested against one of the best in the organization. Rory Baine. Rory was adept at the same forms of martial arts as Hiro. Karate, Tang Soo Do, kickboxing, Kung Fu, Judo, Muay Thai, Jiu-Jitsu, Krav Maga, Aikido, and just for fun, boxing. They sparred for nearly two hours before calling a draw, both men exhausted and unable to continue. It was the sure-fire sign that Hiro made the right choice.

He was finally home.

CHAPTER TWO

The child attempted to cover her ears so as not to hear the screams of the woman lying on the pool table below. It was futile. The sound carried upward against the ceilings of the old building, and she had no choice but to endure.

Two men held the woman's arms down while Demon ripped her clothes from her body. She didn't know his real name, only that he was called Demon by everyone in the club. One of the women said it was because he was a demon straight from hell, whatever that meant.

She'd been here since her pathetic, ill-timed birth. According to Candy, the only woman who ever tried to help her, her mother's car broke down a few miles from the clubhouse, and she'd walked, eight and a half months pregnant, to get help. What she got instead was a nightmare. Despite her pregnancy, she was raped, beaten, and kept naked for the enjoyment of the men around her.

When she went into labor, no one even bothered to check on her. She delivered the child by herself, with only a little help from another woman who looked worse off than she was. Her nightmare was only just beginning. Her daughter was taken from her, sent to a room in another part of the clubhouse to be fed and cared for by someone other than her mother. She was not so fortunate.

Before her body was ready, the men were abusing her again, raping her repeatedly, night after night. She had one escape, only one, and she took it. The knife lying on the bedside table of the man who'd raped her last was too good to overlook. While he got up to use the bathroom, she took the knife and slashed both of her wrists, then stabbed herself in the heart for good measure.

Her last memory was of the man cussing at her for bleeding on his sheets and his booted foot coming toward her dying body.

The child was not as lucky. She wasn't given a name, only referred to as 'girl.' As soon as she was able to walk, she was forced to run errands for the men. She was given no clothing and very little food. A few of the older women tried to protect her, but the punishment brought down on them was too much to bear. She was on her own.

Small and underweight for her age, she tried to hide, but they always found her. When one of the women told her she should try to run away, she was caught, beaten, and placed in the cage above the main floor of the clubhouse. Not even given a bucket for her own waste, she relieved herself through the cage and onto the floor, where another young girl was forced to clean up after her.

Covering her ears, she tried to block out the screams of the poor woman on the table below, but they were too loud. The fourth man to thrust himself into the woman was angry because he said he couldn't get hard enough. He slapped her several times, then gripping the pool stick, he began violating her body.

When the cries stopped, she uncovered her ears only to hear laughing below her. The woman was still lying on the table, her legs spread open, her eyes wide with shock. Her naked body was bruised and battered. Yet no one cared. She was insignificant, unimportant. None of these men cared whether the woman lived or died, whether she had family or not. It was as if life would just go on for everyone else.

A few minutes later, two of the younger men entered and carried the body out of the clubhouse. It wasn't the first time, and it wouldn't be the last. The men were violent, abusive men. Not just with women but with one another as well.

She spent most of her nights in the cage above the floor. During the day, she was expected to clean and help cook for the men. One day a woman pulled her into a room and sat her on a bed.

"Do you know what today is?" she asked her. The girl shook her head, confused. "You're thirteen today. It's your birthday. I knew your mother, and she loved you more than anything. You'll be starting your period soon."

"Period?" the girl questioned.

"It's what happens when a young girl becomes a young lady. It means that you can make babies."

"B-but they don't like kids," she whispered to the woman.

"No, they don't. I'm not sure why Demon kept you, but I want to explain what happens, okay?" The girl nodded, listening intently to everything the woman told her. She was frightened at first to learn that she'd bleed, but when the woman told her it happens to all women, and it's normal, she let out a sigh of relief.

"Girl, you need to understand; Demon wants you for his own. Once he thinks you're old enough, he's going to touch you like he touches those other girls." Her eyes went wide with fear, and she shook her head, holding her hands over her ears. "I know. I know, honey, and I wish I could take it away, but I can't. Just remember this. If you ever get a chance to run, take it. Run as fast and as far as you can."

"Girl!"

They heard Demon yell her name, and she rushed from the room toward the sounds. Standing in front of him, he gripped her face, squeezing forcefully until she looked up at him. His disgusting smile made the girl want to vomit, but she stood still, staring at the man.

"Yea, you got them big brown eyes like your mama. I'm gonna enjoy those eyes lookin' up at me when I take you. For now, you can learn to do a few other things," he said. Gripping her upper arm, he practically dragged her to his room, where he sat her on the bed. Stripping off his clothes, the girl tried to look away, but he wouldn't allow it.

"This here is a cock," he grinned. "You need to learn to stroke it, suck it, and eventually take it. You're mine. I own you, and you will do as I ask. Give me your hand."

She tried to scoot away, but his grip was too firm. He pulled her arm, yanking it forcefully, and then pried open her fingers, wrapping them around his hard, long thing he called a cock. He moved her hand up and down on him, but she just looked away. Demon was breathing heavy, grunting, and groaning like the men on the floor at night. She felt a warm, sticky liquid hit her fingers, and she cringed.

"Now you lick it," he laughed. Tears sprang to her eyes as she shook her head. He shoved her hand against her lips, then pried her mouth open. "Lick it!"

Gagging, she ran from the room as he laughed.

"You're mine, Girl, mine!"

It didn't seem possible, but her world only got worse from then on. Demon would make her rub his hard thing in front of the other men, then lick his sticky stuff. Sometimes, when he was feeling generous, he would make her rub other men too.

One night, everything changed. For the worse. They lowered her cage to the floor, forcing her to crawl toward Demon. As she moved, the men slapped her bare behind, some hitting her with their belts, tearing at her skin. She tried not to cry, not to scream. They liked it when you did that.

"It's time, Girl," he said, grinning at her with his tobacco-stained teeth. "Tie her down."

No. No, this could not be happening. She knew what that meant. It only took two men to tie her down to the table while the other men cheered. Demon lowered his pants, pulling out the hard thing that he made her rub. Her eyes went wide with terror as he rubbed against her, then shoved it inside.

She tried not to scream. Really, she did, but it was too much for her tiny body.

"Oh, fuck yea, boys! Fresh meat, tight as a new pair of boots." He grunted and moaned, thrusting inside her tender, young flesh. When he was done, he nodded to another man who did the same. Over and over again her body was abused, and she couldn't even manage tears.

It was one of the oldest of the men who stepped in, taking pity on her young body.

"She's had enough, Demon," he said, staring at her.

"What'd you say?" he growled, glaring at the man who'd dared to tell him what to do.

"She's had enough. You're gonna kill her. Look at her, she's bleedin' everywhere. This was her first time. Give her a minute."

Demon frowned at the other man, taking a few steps toward him as the others watched. The girl curled herself into a ball, shaking from pain and blood loss.

"Don't interfere in my business," he said. "Girl belongs to me. I've made that clear."

"No argument, she belongs to you," said the man. "You just don't want her dead before you train her."

Demon looked back at the tiny body and nodded.

"Candy!"

"Yes," said a woman, running toward them.

"Clean her up. Get her on birth control. I don't need any more unwanted babies around here. She's getting tatted tomorrow."

The woman, Candy, took her to the showers and washed her clean, helping her into her very first nightgown. There wasn't much to it, but it at least covered her upper body.

"It will get better, honey. Just try to please him," she said. When she looked up at the woman, there were tears streaming down her face, and that's when she knew. It wouldn't get better for her. It would never get better for her.

She was tattooed the next day: Property of Demon. She couldn't see it, but she felt it and knew what they'd done. She would never escape. Never. Three more years of repeated beatings, rapes, and tortures. Three long, horrible years before her moment came.

While Demon was trying to stave off an attack by a rival gang, she pulled on the only clothing she owned, packed a loaf of bread, and crawled beneath the fence. She did exactly what the woman had told her to do years before. She ran.

Inside the clubhouse for eighteen years, two months, and twenty-seven days, she wasn't even sure where she was going or where she currently was located. She had no education, no money, and barely spoke to anyone. But she ran.

When she finally stopped in an alleyway behind a pizza parlor, she thought she'd died and gone to heaven. She sat in that alley for almost a week eating the scraps of discarded pizza before the owner asked if she needed help. She was so frightened, she ran.

Along the way, she discovered that she had run from the Arizona-Nevada border all the way to Texas. A police officer pulled over and asked if she needed help. Knowing that they would find her if she didn't hide, she said yes.

For four months, she lived in a shelter for battered women. Four peaceful, warm, quiet months. When she heard the motorcycles, she knew. The loud pipes rattled the windows, and the woman who ran the shelter handed her a bag with a change of clothes, five energy bars, and two hundred dollars.

"Run," she said.

Five years of running from place to place, only to have to leave again because they might find her. Five years of changing her name over and over again. Each place she landed, she expanded her mind. She'd been taught to read, basic math, and even a few words in Spanish.

In north Louisiana, she went to work for a woman that owned her own salon. The woman taught her all about hair and skin. On the weekends, she would help her with her reading, and during the week, she trained her to give facial treatments and to do makeup for the clients.

A year later, with her GED in hand and a new name, Winter Cole, she left to travel south. She wanted to be as far from noise and motorcycle pipes as she could get. The roadside café where she stopped was quiet, and the food was amazing. When the two beautiful women at the table next to her began speaking to her, Winter wasn't sure what to do.

"Sorry, we're kind of chatty," smiled the younger woman. "My name is Keegan, and this is my mother, Tinley."

"Hi," she said quietly. Keegan looked at her mom and frowned. The oversized sweatshirt hung low on one shoulder, and she caught a glimpse of the tattoo and the red scars around it.

"Honey, are you in trouble?" asked Tinley.

"I-I'm not sure," she said, knowing that she was lying to the woman.

"We can help you," said Keegan. "I own a salon near here. Do you need a job?" Winter nodded at the woman, her long brown hair covering her face.

"I can do facials and makeup," she said. "I'm not licensed. I only have my GED."

"That's okay," smiled Keegan. "Will you come with us to see the shop? It's just over there." The girl looked, seeing the sign for the salon, and nodded. As they left the café, passing the motorcycle shop, the girl began to shake, keeping her head down.

"Hey, hey, it's okay," said Keegan. "They're friends. Good men who would never hurt a woman." Winter shook her head, and Tinley sped up, leading her into the salon.

"Honey, you're in trouble, and I've been there," said Tinley. "This is a safe place to be. We have some very special men here who help to protect us and keep others off the property. If you're running, and I suspect that you are, this is the place for you to be. Will you tell me your name?"

"Winter. Winter Cole."

"Is that your real name?" asked Tinley.

"I don't have a real name."

"Okay, Winter is a pretty name. We'll keep that. Is someone looking for you?" She nodded. "Will you tell me who? Our security team needs to know so they can make sure they don't come this way."

"Los Muertos."

"Thank you for telling me that," said Tinley. The door opened, and Eagle and Hawk stepped inside. Their identical faces smiled at their wives, the mother-daughter duo, and then looked at the new face in the room. Instead of looking back at them, she ducked her head and shrunk against the wall. Eagle frowned at Tinley.

"Winter? This is my husband, Eagle O'Neal, and his twin brother, who is married to my daughter, Hawk O'Neal." Winter didn't look up, but Eagle knelt low to the ground.

"Hi, Winter. It's very nice to meet you," he said quietly. "No one will harm you here, honey. No one. Do you have a place to stay?"

"No. I sleep outside," she said.

"It's getting awfully cold," said Hawk, kneeling next to his brother. "We have a place here that you can stay. There's a small efficiency apartment above the salon. It has a sofa bed and a small kitchen. It's not much, but it's clean and safe." She raised her head to stare at the foursome in front of her.

"Nowhere is safe."

CHAPTER THREE

Hiro had been watching the woman for weeks now. She didn't speak to anyone; she barely made any sound at all. It was as if she wanted to remain invisible. When Hiro learned of the tattoo on her back, he knew he had to do something.

"Hi, Riley, Gabi, how are you?" he said, smiling at the two women.

"Hello, Hiro, you cute little thing," smiled Gabi. Hiro only shook his head. He was hardly little, but Gabi had a way of making you feel like a teenager. "What can we do for you, handsome?"

"I was wondering, Winter, she has a tattoo on her back that makes her identifiable."

"That's right," said Riley, frowning at the young man.

"Do we have a laser that can remove it?" he asked.

"No, I'm sorry; we don't. We've just never had a need for it. I've tried to get her to see someone that has one, but she refuses to leave here. You might find those more in plastic surgery or med spa facilities. Why?"

"If we had one, you could remove the tattoo, right?" Gabi and Riley frowned at Hiro but nodded. "And then Keegan could use it in the spa, right?"

"Hiro, I think it's wonderful that you're asking about this," said Gabi, "but those machines are expensive. Really good ones can be over a hundred grand."

"I have money. Buy one."

"Hiro..." whispered Riley.

"Please. Buy one and remove her tattoo." He waited patiently as Riley looked at Gabi and then back at Hiro.

"Alright, Hiro. I'll do some research and see how quickly we can get one in here. It's a wonderful thing you're doing, Hiro. That young woman deserves a chance, and this will help her."

It was another week before the machine arrived, and Riley explained what they were able to do.

"It's going to hurt, Winter. It may take several treatments, but it will be gone permanently from your body. There might be a little scarring or rough skin, but the ink will be gone."

"Why are you doing this?" she asked, staring at the women. Gabi looked at her frightened face and wanted to punch the man that beat this woman down.

"We aren't really doing it," said Gabi. "Hiro bought the machine. For the spa, but also for you."

"For me? Why? Why would he do that? What does he want?" she asked, suddenly feeling a panic rise in her chest.

"Winter, he doesn't want anything except for you to be happy and have a normal, healthy life," said Riley. "If you're ready, we'll do the first treatment and see what it looks like after that."

The tattoo had been so poorly done it only took two treatments to remove completely. Seeing the white, scaley skin in the mirror, she nodded at the doctors and then left the room. Riley looked at Gabi and shook her head.

"I think what Hiro did was the kindest thing I've ever seen, but I'm not sure she has the emotional maturity to appreciate it."

"It doesn't matter," said Gabi. "He didn't do it to be appreciated. That's what makes it all the more special."

Winter walked the long drive between the massive trees, pulling her sweater tighter around her body. She tried to speak to the others. Really, she did, but speaking usually got her beaten. So far, the men and women had been kind to her. The woman, Alexandra, had given her clothes that fit her tiny body, and now, with the tattoo removed, she felt just a little safer.

But they would come for her. Demon would find her, beat her, rape her, make her crawl to touch him and the other men. She shook with fear and cold but kept walking slowly toward the river.

Cam watched Winter out of the corner of his eye as she made her way inside the cafeteria. Kate and Ajei sat next to their husbands, and Ajei followed Cam's gaze toward Winter.

"She's the saddest woman I've ever met," said Ajei softly. "It's not just sadness, it's sheer terror of anything and everything that moves. Riley and Rachelle convinced her to let us do a physical on her before we removed her tattoo. It's the worst case of abuse I've ever seen. I can't even begin to give you the details. I think if we could just get her to sit down and hear what happened to people like Rachelle, Alexandra, Ace, we have so many that have been through traumatic experiences, it would help her."

"Can you tell us anything, baby?" asked Luke.

"I can tell you that she was abused more than anyone on this property and for a very long period of time. It was brutal, sick, and disgusting. She's terrified of loud noises, animals, most of the women, and obviously all of you."

"That doesn't help us much, Ajei," said Cam.

"Cam, I love you, but what happened to that poor woman is not something I want to let anyone know about without her permission. She has been abused since the day she was born, and I am not exaggerating that. The. Day. She. Was born."

"Hey," said Kate quietly, "look. Hiro's speaking with her."

"Good morning, Winter," said Hiro, standing a few feet from the table. She looked up and then back down at her food.

"Good morning," she whispered.

"Good morning, Hiro," he grinned. She stared at him; her head cocked to the side. "Remember? My name is Hiro."

"I-I remember," she said, nodding. "I'm so sorry."

"No, no, that's not what I meant. You don't have to use my name if you don't want to. It's a weird name, isn't it? I mean, it sounds like I'm calling myself a hero, h-e-r-o, not my name, Hiro, H-i-r-o. It's actually Hirohito, but Hiro for short. What can I say? My parents did it to me." He smiled, trying to make her feel more comfortable.

She stared at him as Keegan and Hawk waited for her to respond to him. Keegan smiled up at Hiro, trying to encourage him to continue.

"Winter? I was wondering if you might help me with something," he said softly. She looked at him, a mix of fear and interest passing across her face. "Mama Irene is very big on Mardi Gras, the celebration that comes before the beginning of Lent. It's about a month away, but they enter a boat in the floating parade every year. I've been tasked with coming up with a theme and decorating the boat. I could sure use your artistic eye."

Winter looked at Keegan and Hawk, then back at Hiro. She wondered what the man was trying to do. What is his game?

"I'm not artistic," she said, shaking her head.

"Yes, you are," said Keegan. "The way you do makeup is an artist's touch, Winter. I've never seen anything like it. You make women glow."

"You could do the same thing with the boat. Look, there's no pressure at all. It just might be fun for you. The boat would be visible here on the property, right there at the dock. Everyone could see you, and I promise I won't come near you or touch you," said Hiro.

"You'd have to come near me if we were on the boat," she said, looking at him. Hiro took one small step closer to the table. Winter sucked in a breath but didn't jump, so that was progress.

"Winter, I'm not sure how to explain this to you again, but I will not hurt you. It is not within me as a man to hurt you. I would sooner kill myself than do anything to harm you. I will do my very, very best to not come near you on that boat, but you are right. We would be in close proximity. If there is anything I can do to make you feel more comfortable, just tell me. I'll make sure that you see me at all times; I'll leave any weapons on the dock; I'll try not to talk to you. I just would love a good partner for this project, and I think you can do it."

Winter looked at the handsome man. She knew in her heart that he was different from the men she'd known in her life. For one, he had the kindest eyes of anyone she'd ever seen, and she'd seen evil eyes in her short lifetime. He had no tattoos on his body, and his hair wasn't greasy or dirty. He was muscular, but from fitness, not from brawling.

"Can I think about it?" she asked. Hiro flashed her a big smile.

"Yes. You can think about it. I'm going into town to get supplies, but maybe we could talk about this tomorrow evening at dinner if you'll allow me to join the table. If you have ideas, I'd love to hear them." She looked at Keegan and Hawk, wondering if they would be there.

"We'd love for you to join us, brother," said Hawk.

"I've never been to Mardi Gras," she said, looking at him. "I don't know what it's supposed to look like."

"I'll send some pictures to Keegan's e-mail address. You can take a look at the boats they've done in the past. Until then, I'm very happy you're going to think about this. I hope you have a good day, Winter. Remember that you can call me or any of the men here for help if you ever need it."

"Thank you. You, too, I mean, you have a good day, too." Hiro turned and left, joining the others for breakfast.

"He's a very good man, Winter," said Hawk. "He was in the military for a number of years, and his instincts are to protect, not to hurt. Every man you see here is here to protect, not to hurt."

"Keegan told me," she said quietly.

"I know she told you, Winter, but I don't think you believe it yet. I wish you'd tell us how we get you to believe us. We want you to stay here. We want to keep you safe, but we can't do that if you don't tell us what we're up against. We know it's Los Muertos, but details would be helpful."

She shook her head, tears coming to her eyes once again.

"You'll all hate me."

"Okay, enough for now," said Keegan. "Hawk, I'll see you tonight. Winter, let's get to the salon. We have a full book today." The other woman nodded and walked toward the door.

"Baby, I didn't mean to upset her, but she has to…"

"No, she doesn't have to, Hawk. She may just leave one night without telling any of us, and where does that leave her? She will die if she leaves here. I know it in my heart. Please, don't push her. Back off and let this happen in her time." Hawk nodded, kissing his wife as she followed Winter out the door.

"No luck?" asked Cam from behind him.

"Fucking nothing."

CHAPTER FOUR

Winter was surprised that George had fulfilled his promise of making her favorite foods. Hamburgers, French fries, and chocolate cake with thick chocolate icing. It was wonderful. She savored every bite, enjoying the meal more than she cared to admit. Being deprived of food so many times throughout her life only made her appreciate meals like this all the more.

What she didn't expect was for George to announce that they were her favorites, and everyone would thank her for the meal. She saw their smiles, but the roar of approval and thunderous applause crumbled her. Covering her ears, she shrunk back against the wall, making herself as small as she possibly could.

The cheers. The cheers of men laughing and egging others on to touch her, rape her, put objects inside her. The cheers wouldn't go away. It all came flooding back. The hands touching her, the smell of body odor and liquor. It was drowning her.

"Winter? Winter, it's Hiro. Look at me, honey. Look up at me. It's alright. Everything is okay," he said quietly. She lowered her hands, her hair still covering her face, and Hiro's heart cracked a little more.

"I'm so sorry, child," said George. She shook her head but was unable to say a word.

"Winter, I'm going to lift you off the floor now, okay?" He thought she nodded but couldn't tell. Gently, he slid one arm beneath her legs, the other around her back, and lifted her easily. "I'm going to take you to your cottage now."

Hiro walked slowly with Winter in his arms as the cold winds bit into their skin. The efficiency above the spa left Winter feeling alone and frightened, so Mama Irene and the others convinced her to take one of the cottages. At least here, she was surrounded by people that could help her if she needed it. When he was standing outside her cottage, he gently began to set her down, but she held tightly to his neck.

"It's okay, Winter. We'll just sit on the porch for a minute." Hiro sat on the swing, grabbing the blanket hanging over the back, and covered them both, gently moving his feet to make a slow glide. He didn't say anything. He didn't reach for her again. He just sat quietly next to her, gently swinging his feet.

"I'll never be able to face them again," she whispered, looking off into the distance. Hiro noticed that she rarely cried. She might scream or cover her ears, but she never let tears fall.

"Yes, you will," said Hiro. "They felt terrible for making you feel frightened, but in their defense, Winter, none of us knows what frightens you and what doesn't."

"Everything," she said, looking at him. "Everything frightens me. I know enough to know that's not normal. I'm not smart, but I'm not stupid either."

He nodded thoughtfully, wondering if that were an exaggeration. Again, he waited patiently, hoping that she would open up to him more. She opened her mouth a few times but said nothing. Hiro was going to wait her out.

"I never thanked you for getting the laser to remove my tattoo. Riley and Gabi told me you did it. I don't understand why. Why did you do that?"

"I'm glad you got it done," he said, staring off into the night. "As for why, I did it because you deserve to have a chance at a normal life, Winter. I know you don't see it now but staying here will give you that chance. That tattoo would only hold you back. It would be a reminder of your old life."

"They made me get it. They held me down and forced me to get it. When they were done, they raped me and beat me because I didn't sit still. When they finished, they did it again." She looked at Hiro, waiting a moment before continuing.

"I won't tell you everything. I can't tell you everything, but I will explain what happened in there," she said, looking down at her feet. "From the time I was a little girl, the men at the Los Muertos club, they would bring women out on the floor and do things to them in front of everyone. Horrible, painful, awful things. They would cheer really loudly, yelling for the men to go further, to do more, and then there would be this loud roar of applause. The more she cried, the more she begged to be released, the louder they got.

"When they all clapped in there, it was as if I were in that clubhouse again, seeing those women… being one of those women. I learned to be silent. Not to cry. Not to beg. Not to say anything. I think they hated me more for that." She whispered the last few words, and Hiro's head jerked to see her face. He swallowed, trying to regain his composure.

"Whatever happened, Winter, it wasn't your fault. You've been here for weeks now. You know that we will not harm you. We would never harm you. We only want to help you. I think we've all proven that time and time again. We… I would really love it if you would just trust us, even a little."

"I know," she said, nodding, "which only makes my behavior even worse. You've all been so kind and patient with me. Kinder and more patient than you should have to be. I don't want to be like this, Hiro. I don't want to be afraid all of the time. I don't want to worry that someone will come and get me."

"No one will come and get you," he said, looking at her. "We can stop them, Winter. I know you don't understand that right now, but I need you to trust me. If you trust no one else, trust me, we will stop them. No one will come for you."

She stood from the swing, neatly folding the blanket, placing it over the back once again. She walked to her door, opening the locks with her keys.

"Someone will. One day, someone will come for me."

CHAPTER FIVE

The women all stood at the cafeteria windows watching as Winter shuffled down the tree-lined main road from the big house to the river. Her head was down, the cascade of brunette draped over her face as if hiding. Rachelle turned to the other women in the group, wiping the tears from her face.

"We have to try to reach her," said Rachelle. "If we don't, she's going to break into a million pieces at some point, and we won't be able to put her back together."

"What do you propose?" asked Sophia, staring at the other women in their support group.

Twice a month, the women met for coffee and pastries, but mostly to ensure they were all still on the path to healing. Included in their group were the women who'd experienced the most violent sexual and brutal crimes. Sophia, Rachelle, Alexandra, Noelle, Gray, Rose, Lissa, Lauren, Tory, Cait, Kelsey, Lily, Ashley, Piper, Grace, Taylor, Tinley, Evie, and Marie. Nineteen of the bravest, smartest, most amazing women that any of them knew.

They were seated around the tables watching as Winter was simply biding her time. Biding time until what, they weren't sure, but she was definitely a woman that might bolt at any given moment.

"Rachelle, maybe we need to explain a little bit to the group," said Ashley, turning to look at the other women. "You have to understand that we're bound by patient-doctor confidentiality, but we've always taken the approach of sharing with others on our team. The problem is that I don't think Winter sees herself as part of the team yet. The one person who she's truly connected with is Hiro."

"I'm not comfortable sharing a lot about her situation," said Rachelle. "Ashley and Bree are the true trauma specialists, but I will tell you that there's a reason we've treated her with kid gloves. We all have stories of our horrific attacks and abuse. What was done to her is beyond what any of us can possibly imagine."

"Dear God," murmured Sophia. "Worse than any of us?"

"Worse," said Rachelle. "I mean, if there's such a thing as less worse or more worse. It's all horrific, but for some of Winter's, she was just a child."

"Why is Ace walking toward her?" asked Lily.

"Ace can relate to Winter on a level we cannot. Some of you know that Ace was kept in a cage in a closet as a child. He was tormented, poked at, made fun of, and denied personal needs. Someone saved him when he was just a boy, but no one saved that girl," said Bree.

"She was kept in a cage?" asked Cait. Rachelle, Ashley, and Bree stared at one another. Rachelle finally nodded, then spoke.

"She was kept in a cage hanging above the main floor of the motorcycle club, where everyone could watch whatever torture was delivered that day, and where she was forced to watch others. She was branded, beaten, forced to perform sexual favors on men old enough to be her grandfather. Her first sexual experience was rape. Tied to a pool table."

"No," whispered Sophia as she shook her head. "No, please tell me someone saved that child."

"She's here. Whether or not she's saved is another story," said Bree, frowning at the image through the window. The women all turned their chairs, watching as their once completely withdrawn Ace walked beside the woman.

"Hello," said Ace softly, standing about ten feet from Winter. She turned with a fright, staring at the man. She knew his name and knew that he was one of the men on the property, but that didn't mean that she trusted him.

"Hello."

"May I walk with you? Sometimes, my head gets all scrambled staring at the computers and listening as our men complete their missions." She nodded, still cautiously staring at him. "Hiro is fine, by the way. They'll be a little longer than we thought, but he's fine. Our men are the best at what they do, Winter. We help those that can't help themselves. We save women and children from trafficking rings; we stop drugs from getting to our streets; we help the helpless. We don't harm them. Not ever."

She nodded again, taking very small steps.

"It's beautiful here, isn't it? I was on a team with Ghost and the boys at the motorcycle shop..." Her head popped up as if he'd pointed a weapon at her. "They're all good men, Winter. They build the motorcycles because they're good at it, and it brings in considerable revenue for our organization. They were part of an elite Special Forces team that consisted of SEALs, Rangers, Marines, and Coast Guard. Not one of those men has ever laid hands in anger on a woman or child. Never. Yes, they like to ride, so do I, but we're not all bad."

Silence met his gaze once more, and she turned slowly, walking again. Ace took it as a sign to continue.

"As I was saying, I came with Ghost and the others several years ago. Before that, I was in the Navy. I was with Navy Intelligence and provided information to Ghost and his men that would help them complete their missions." She looked at him questioningly, and he nodded. "As we've told you before, everyone here is former military.

"But before that, before joining this team and finding my beautiful wife, Charlie, I was like you, Winter." He noticed her sideways glance at him and kept talking. "My parents were horrid people. They kept me locked in a cage in the closet most of the time. When they were feeling generous, they pulled me out of the closet and let their sick friends poke at me and throw things at me.

"One night, this couple seemed to have a conscience. They couldn't stand it and left, reporting it to the police. This amazing policeman rescued me and eventually adopted me. He was the best man I'd ever known. When I first went to live with him, I couldn't sleep in a bed." Ace knew from Mama Irene that Winter wasn't sleeping in her bed either. He hoped his story would help.

"I'd only ever had the floor or the cage. He would lay with me on the floor, never touching me, never yelling at me. He would just bring in a pillow and blanket and lay next to me. Then he got me involved in track and field, computers, everything. He supported me no matter what I did or where I went. It took me years to let anyone come near me or touch me.

"Ghost was the first man, other than my father, I trusted, allowing him to shake my hand and eventually hug me. Charlie really changed my life. My world changed with the kindness of that police officer, my father, and with Ghost. Two men, Winter. Two fine, courageous men who both rode motorcycles.

"I don't know your story, honey. But I've lived at least a small part of it. I've contemplated taking my own life." Her head jolted up as if to deny his statement, but she said nothing. "I've contemplated running. I've even contemplated killing them, although they're both dead now. None of it would have made me feel any less pain.

"The pain is what drives you to where you need to be, Winter. I know that's hard to understand right now, but if you could just see clear to trust the people here, the people who want to help you, your life would get there. They can help to get you to a place where you can trust those around you, here on this property, and live a beautiful, wonderful, happy life. It won't ever go away completely. It can't. It's inside of you. But we can help you."

She stopped beneath the live oaks, the wind whipping her curtain of brunette hair over her face. It was as if she didn't have the strength to brush it away.

"They'll find me. I'll have to run again."

"Again?" asked Ace, frowning at the woman. "They've found you before?" Winter nodded.

"But I heard them coming, and I ran. I just ran and ran and ran. I had nothing. I begged for food, begged. I had no clothing, no car, no money, but I ran. I should have run sooner. I should have done a lot of things sooner."

"Stop running, Winter. Let us help you. If you trust us, if you like being here with Keegan and Tinley and George and Mary and even Hiro, if you want to be here, trust us to fix this for you."

"Thank you for talking to me," she said, her head lowered once more. "I'm tired now."

Ace just nodded with a small smile, watching the young woman walk back toward her cottage. He'd fill Hiro in on his conversation when he returned, but until then, he'd keep watch over the woman.

"Well?" said Ghost, stepping closer to him.

"She didn't even blink an eye when I told her what happened to me. That only tells me that her hell was far worse than mine. What she did say that was helpful was that they'd found her once before. I think we need to get seriously proactive on this and find those bastards before they find her."

"We need to know specifically who we're looking for, Ace. You know that. We can't wipe out an entire motorcycle club."

"Can't we?" smirked Ace. "We've done it before, and we'll do it again for less worthy causes than Winter." Ghost nodded, staring down at his friend.

"Find them."

CHAPTER SIX

Hiro was humming a silly tune as he worked on the party barge for the Mardi Gras parade. Every once in a while, he'd look toward Winter, her waterfall of brown hair covering her face. He felt her eyes on him a time or two, but he couldn't tell if it was interest or if she were simply watching to be sure he kept his distance.

The cold was still hovering over the property. The rain had held off, but the wind whipped across the bow, Winter's hair flying with it. She struggled to push it back, but it was so long and thick she couldn't get it to stay in place. He stood, taking slow, careful steps toward her.

"Winter? The wind is pretty bad out here. Would you allow me to use the ribbon to tie back your hair?" She stared at him for a moment, unsure of whether to run or not. He didn't move; he didn't attempt to force her. He just stared at her with a kind, sweet gaze. Finally, she nodded.

Hiro stood behind the woman and gently ran his fingers through the thick strands, pulling back her abundant, silky hair. He wrapped the ribbon around the heavy ponytail, then tied it tightly. Staring at the back of her head and neck, he swallowed, wanting to scream out. There were scars in the shape of bite marks behind her ears. The tip of her left ear appeared to be bitten off or cut off. He moved around to face her.

"There," he smiled. "Now I can see your beautiful face, and you don't have to keep fighting the wind."

"I'm not beautiful," she said, shaking her head.

"I think you are," said Hiro, casually shrugging. "I think almost everyone has beauty inside them. You have to find it and show it to others. Sometimes, it's hard. Sometimes, it's easy. But it's not the outside that makes you truly beautiful. It's what you have on the inside. Your heart and soul."

Winter continued to weave the ribbons and beads together, making a bunting for the side rails of the boat. Hiro sat on the deck, cutting the strips of ribbons, his legs crossed beneath him. He was starting to get a good pulse on Winter and could tell when she was building to say something. With his infinite patience, he just continued to do the work, glancing her way every few minutes.

"I didn't know my mother," she said quietly. Hiro didn't move. He simply looked up at her. "One of the women at the club told me that her car broke down, and she walked for help. She was eight months pregnant with me. They didn't care. They raped her, beat her, and forced her to deliver her own baby. The woman said she thought they hoped I would die during birth, but when I didn't, they gave me to another woman. Then, they used my mom only a few hours after giving birth to me."

Hiro closed his eyes, taking a slow deep breath. Unimaginable cruelty. Those were the words floating through his brain.

"I don't even know what she looked like. I don't know if she had brown hair or brown eyes or if she looked completely different."

"Do you know her name?" asked Hiro. Winter looked up at him and shook her head.

"No one knew her name. No one cared."

"I'll bet that someone cared," said Hiro. "Someone out there lost their daughter or sister, or maybe even wife. I'm sure we could try…"

"He made me touch him," she whispered. "I was a child, and he made me touch him."

Hiro looked up at her, her face void of any expression whatsoever. Her dark eyes were filled with sadness, yet she didn't know how to let it go. The only life she knew was a life of pain and shame. She'd never learned to cry as a child or to tell someone when something was painful. All the things that normal children took for granted, Winter was deprived of.

"You can cry, you know," said Hiro. She stared at him for a moment, then shook her head. "No one will think poorly of you, no one. You can cry, you can scream, you can yell, you can even throw things if it makes you feel better. You can even throw things at me. I don't mind. Everyone needs to do it now and then."

"If I cried, they liked it. They wanted me to cry or scream for help, so I refused."

"I won't like it. I'll hate it. It will break my heart to see you cry or scream, but if it makes you feel better, I'll sit right here and let you cry," he said.

Winter wasn't even sure she knew how to cry. Her tears were forced from pain and torture. Bringing tears on to vent wasn't something she was familiar with doing.

"I can scream?" she asked.

"As loud as you want."

"Y-you won't hit me?"

"Never. Never will I hit you." Hiro stood up and held out his hand to her. She stared at it, then allowed him to pull her to her feet.

Standing on the deck of the boat, Winter looked around. Off in the distance, near the cafeteria, there were men milling about. She saw a few people walking in the gardens, but no one was close. She opened her mouth and let out a short squeal that sounded forced and restrained.

"Come on," he grinned, "you can do better than that. Scream, Winter. For all the pain, the anger, for everything you went through, just scream. Let it all out."

Opening her mouth once more, she screamed as loudly as anyone Hiro had ever heard. It was short, but it was a loud scream. He noticed a few heads turning but held up his hand, casually letting them know it was all okay.

"Again."

Winter's body was shaking with the need to be rid of her anger. It was as if she could no longer control it. She screamed and screamed until she was kneeling on the deck, rocking back and forth with her arms wrapped around her waist. Tears flooded her face as Hiro knelt beside her.

"May I hug you?" he asked sweetly. She nodded, leaning forward until her head was against his shoulder. Hiro sat cross-legged, pulling her onto his lap, and hugged her, rocking her back and forth. Dom, Rory, and Aiden stepped onto the boat, followed by Rachelle and Mama Irene.

"Winter? Are you alright? What can we do?" asked Rory.

She looked up at the big man, shaking her head. She screamed again, and they all jumped back at the horrendous sound of a wounded animal. Rory wasn't a man prone to emotions, but this woman was breaking his heart. That sound, the sound of pain and fear and loss, was unlike anything he'd ever heard before.

"They raped me!" she yelled. "They raped me all the time!"

"We know, honey," said Hiro, hugging her tightly. "We know. It won't happen again. We would never allow it to happen again."

"They raped me and beat me and p-put things inside me! It didn't matter if I cried or screamed. They did it to all of the women. They killed women and just left them for me to see from my cage."

"Child," said Mama Irene, kneeling down beside her, "it's not your fault. It's not your fault."

"Why? Why do men hurt women?" she asked, looking from Hiro to Dom to Rory. "Why do you enjoy it?"

"No man here enjoys hurting a woman," said Dom. "No one. We make sure that men who hurt women are not long for this world, Winter. Not all men are bad. Not all men hurt. You had the unfortunate path of finding a group of men who do enjoy it."

"Why can't I be normal?" she cried into Hiro's shoulder.

"You are the most normal woman I know," he said, lifting her chin. "Yes, you've had a horrible experience in your life. The worst. But you are normal, and if you'll allow us to help you, we can make sure that it only gets better from here. It won't go away, Winter. It will always be in your memory, but one day you will wake up, and it won't be the first memory."

By now, Tailor, Alec, Max, and Gaspar were standing behind Dom and Rory, having heard her screams from their vantage point. Aiden helped Mama Irene off the floor as Hiro stood with Winter. She looked at Mama Irene and back at the men.

"Are they all your sons? Are you their mother?"

"They are. Not all by blood, but they're mine all the same. I treat everyone here like my child or grandchild, including you," she said proudly.

"Do they lie? Do they hurt women?"

"Never," she said resolutely.

Winter was shaking so desperately they thought she might break into pieces. One painful step at a time, she walked toward the wall of testosterone, staring up at them. It was the bravest thing she'd ever done. She looked at Rory first.

"You would never hurt a woman? As big as you are, as strong, you would never ever hurt a woman?" she asked quietly.

"Never in my entire life," he replied. She looked up at Alec and Tailor.

"Have you… have you ever forced a woman… made her…"

"Never," said Tailor. "No man does that and lives, not here, not around us. None. Love is different, Winter. Love between a man and a woman is consensual. You agree to touch one another, love one another. Rape is forced and violent. It's not about love. It's not even about sex. It's about power."

"Power," she whispered.

"That's right, honey," said Alec. "Men who rape are seeking power. They want power over their victims. Don't give him that. Don't give any of them that. Take the power that you deserve and that rightly belongs to you."

Winter slowly turned and saw something in Hiro's face she'd never seen before. Hope. It was as if he were hoping this was a breakthrough. She looked at Mama Irene and then back over her shoulder at the other men.

"I want to scream again," she said to the older woman. Rachelle smiled at her, nodding.

"Let's do it together. I could use a good scream."

Mama Irene's wrinkled hands reached for the younger woman, holding on tightly, as they both let out a loud scream. The men smiled, watching the spectacle. They screamed again and again until Winter was hoarse. She looked at Mama Irene and leaned forward, lowering her head.

Irene knew exactly what to do. She pushed the loose strands of hair from her face and kissed her forehead, then gently, ever so slowly, she pulled her into her arms for a soft hug.

"Are you done?" smiled Hiro. She gave him the smallest, faintest smile and nodded.

"For now."

CHAPTER SEVEN

"I'm going to take a shower and get ready for dinner," said Winter, rising from the deck of the boat. She'd just finished the last of the bunting and stored it inside the covered space below deck.

"Alright," said Hiro, nodding at her. "I enjoyed our time together today, Winter. Thank you for telling me a piece of your story."

Stepping onto the dock, she turned to look up at him. His sincere expression nearly floored her. She'd never had anyone care for her, ask her about herself. Never.

"I've never in my life had anyone as nice to me as you are, as all of you are. I know I'm not expressing my gratitude very well, but I do thank you, Hiro."

"No gratitude needed, Winter. This is how we treat everyone in our family." She gave him a strange look and started to leave, then turned to face him once again.

"If you'd like to come by my cottage at six, we'll talk some more before dinner."

"I will be there at five-fifty-nine," he grinned. She tilted her head.

"I believe I said six." Hiro was confused, and then the tiniest of smiles touched her lips.

"Did you just make a joke with me? Oh, my God! Winter Cole just made a joke with me," he laughed.

"Six, Hiro," she said, walking away. She didn't realize it until she was inside her cottage, but she still had a big smile on her face and felt better than she had in years.

Hiro finished picking up all the materials, neatly stacking them inside the wheelhouse. As he stepped off the boat, Dom, Rory, Aiden, Alec, Tailor, Max, and Gaspar were waiting for him. Luke and Cam were walking toward them as well.

"Am I in trouble?" he asked.

"No, brother, we wanted to let you know that what you did for that young woman was nothing short of miraculous. Rachelle said she'd been trying to get a break-through like that for weeks now," said Gaspar. "I'm not sure what magic you have, Hiro, but you're doing well by that girl."

"The things they did to her," he said, shaking his head. "I don't understand men like that. She said that her mother was eight months pregnant with her when her car broke down, and she walked to their clubhouse for help. They didn't give a shit, raping and beating her until she was in labor. They left her alone to deliver Winter on her own, then handed her off to another woman to care for. They started raping her mother again right away."

"Fucking hell," growled Alec. "I want to get my hands on these men."

"You may have a chance," said Ghost, walking toward them. "Ace had a conversation with Winter a few days ago. They've followed her for years now. By all accounts, she ran away when she was about eighteen or nineteen. She says she's twenty-five now. Six years that girl has been running. Six."

"What do we know?" asked Cam.

"Los Muertos is the worst of a one-percenter. Even the roughest clubs don't rape, beat, and kill women and children randomly. Their leader, Demon, has been there a long time. He took over for his grandfather after he killed his own father."

"Nice guy," muttered Tailor.

"He's psychotic. According to some people Ace reached out to, he sees nothing wrong with treating women the way Winter was treated. It's been going on for years. When a Los Muertos finds a woman he wants as his, he brands her or tattoos her, and then she belongs to him. But, and this is the big but, Demon gets to have a crack at her if he wants."

"He fucks their women?" asked Dom.

"Yes. With or without permission. He's been known to take girls as young as thirteen or fourteen."

"Winter said he made her touch him when she was just a child," said Hiro. He swallowed hard, staring at the men. "Who does that?"

"It's not something any of us can comprehend, Hiro," said Alec.

"Sh-she said they raped her, but they also put things in her," he frowned.

"The man I spoke with said that bodies that have been found were clearly raped and beaten with pool cues, baseball bats, beer bottles, anything they could get their hands on," said Ghost. "Something you all need to be aware of is that they're in Louisiana."

"What?" growled Cam and Gaspar at the same time.

"They're looking for our girl. If we tell her that, she's going to freak the fuck out. I've asked Keegan to tell her that there was a pipe that burst in the salon, and it will be closed for a few weeks. That should keep her on-property and away from them.

"But. We need to go after them. Make it territorial or something, but my vote is we hop on those bikes and make our way to them and not wait for them to come to us."

"How many?" asked Luke.

"Right now, they have seven men here. They sent their road captain and a few others to scope out the area. I'm not sure if that's to expand or if it's because of Winter, but either way, we have to get them to back off."

"Where are they?" asked Hiro.

"I was afraid you were going to ask that," grinned Ghost. "They're at a bar on the other side of the lake. We've got bikes ready for you. Frank, Dom, Keith, Skull, and Razor will go with you. Don't lone wolf this bullshit, Hiro. You're part of a team."

"I know," he said, nodding. He looked at his watch and frowned. "Will you tell Winter I'll be a few minutes late for dinner?"

"I'll tell her, brother," smiled Luke. He nodded.

"Let's go. I'm feeling the need to exercise."

***

The Rust Bucket was a typical biker bar. The floors were sticky, the countertops were sticky, the beer was warm, and the smell was atrocious. The men of Los Muertos had been sitting in this place for three days waiting to see if anyone would come forward about Girl or force them out of their territory.

"Another beer," he growled at the bartender. "Don't you have women in this fucking place? I need my dick sucked."

"You can buy all the dick sucking you want on Bourbon," said the bartender. "Women don't come in here."

He grunted, rubbing the patch on his chest that said Road Captain. His men were seated behind him, their dirty leather matching their dirty bodies. Usually, when they travelled, they would use another club's facility, but lately, Los Muertos wasn't exactly making friends. Ratchet knew their reputation. Although feared, they were also seen as pariahs within the biking community. Hell, they couldn't even get into Daytona any longer thanks to Demon and his fucked-up ways.

He heard the sounds of bikes and turned to look at his boys. These were big bikes, with big, loud pipes, at least six.

"Give me five minutes alone," said Hiro as he stepped off the motorcycle.

"Hiro, we're a team, brother," said Dom. "Going in alone is suicide."

"Naw," he smiled. "Five minutes, then you guys come in."

"No," said Skull. "I'm going in with you. I won't do anything unless you need me to, but we're going in together."

Hiro frowned, but Dom reluctantly nodded as Hiro stepped inside the dark bar, Skull on his heels. Skull took a seat at the end of the bar, and Hiro scanned the room.

Immediately, he knew the seven men that he needed to focus on. They were all out of shape, probably carrying weapons, and slow as Christmas, thanks to their guts and the beer.

One man in particular stared at him as he stepped up to the bar.

"Beer," he said calmly.

The bartender stared at him a moment, then back at Ratchet. He nodded and pulled the beer, sliding it to Hiro. The man standing at the bar with the leather kutte moved closer to him, staring at him, up and down.

"I don't think you belong in here, Chinaman," grinned the man. His teeth, what was left of them, were tobacco-stained, the crudely created tattoos littering his arms and chest. The heavy leather vest he wore had a patch claiming he was the road captain. Hiro simply smiled at the man.

"I'm not Chinese," grinned Hiro. "If you were an educated man, you'd know that." The other man frowned at him, the room suddenly quiet.

"See, Chinese men look slightly different. The structure of their faces is very different, and the eyes, the eyes really give it away." The man stared at him, looking back at his friends with a confused expression.

"I don't give a fuck where you're from. You don't belong here."

"Well, this is a public place. A bar that's open to anyone who wants to enter and buy a beer. I'm part of the public, I have money, and I want a beer, plus my club lives here. You do not," said Hiro.

"You're slow, Chinaman."

"I've told you…"

"Yea, yea, you're not Chinese. I don't give a fuck. Get out, or I'm going to throw you out." Hiro laughed so loud the man in front of him jumped. There were six other men in the room, Hiro literally counting them with his finger, but they didn't matter to him.

"Seven to one," he smiled, looking back at Skull as if to say 'stay out of this.' "Okay, let's do this." The men stared at him, but when the door opened behind him, they all frowned, taking a step back. Hiro turned and shook his head.

"Really? You couldn't give me ten minutes alone with them?" he asked. Frank, Dom, Razor, and Keith grinned.

"Keith was getting nervous and hungry. We won't interfere. We're just here to make sure it's all equal. Go ahead, brother. We'll just sit here and watch." Dom looked at the bartender and slapped the bar. "Three beers and a water."

"You're gonna die, Chinaman," said the man. Hiro reached across the barstool and gripped the man's neck, his thumb pressing artfully into his larynx. The man tried to speak, tried to cry out, but he couldn't. Nothing on his body would move. When Hiro released him, he crumbled to the floor, his windpipe crushed, as he gasped for air, the last breaths leaving his body.

Hiro jerked his head from side to side, the loud cracking echoing in the room. Staring at the men in front of him, he mentally took note of who would be first and who would be last.

"Alright, boys, let's get this done."

"What sort of kung fu shit was that?" said one of the other men of Los Muertos.

"Not kung fu," said Hiro, rolling his eyes. "Look, it's simple. You're in our territory, and you need to leave. Now. If you don't, I'll bring two hundred men to burn down every fucking clubhouse you own. Simple." Hiro saw it coming. He knew it before the man even left his seat. His eyes darted toward Hiro and back to the other three men, then he charged toward him, his shoulder lowered.

Hiro only laughed, dodging out of his way as his body hit the stool next to Keith. Keith's six-feet-five of muscle stood. Lifting his leg, he shoved the man aside.

"Hurry up, Hiro, I'm hungry."

"You're always hungry," laughed Hiro.

The embarrassed man stood, looking from Keith to Hiro, trying to determine which were better odds. Apparently, he thought size mattered. In this case, it did not. As he charged toward Hiro once more, a man behind Hiro came toward him.

Hiro artfully swung his leg around, connecting with the man's jaw in a sickening crunch as he dropped to the floor. In a split second, he turned to see his charging bull come at him again. Raising his knee, he caught the man in the groin, then slammed the heel of his hand into his nose, swinging his elbow into his throat.

"Three down," he smiled, turning to the other four men. "Who's next?"

One of the men started to pull a pistol from his jeans, then felt the sting of a knife in the back of his hand. Hiro turned, expecting to see Dom or Frank as the thrower. Instead, it was Trak standing beside Alec and Tailor.

"What the fuck are those?" said one of the bikers.

"Now that wasn't nice at all," said Tailor. "Ain't nothin' but a good ole country boy. A country boy that likes to break bones."

"We ain't got no beef with you," said the biker. "Chinaman needs to go."

"He's not Chinese," said Trak, staring at the man. He casually walked toward them, pulling his knife from the back of the other man's hand. "I need this back."

"You need to leave. Now," said Alec. "This is our territory, and you didn't ask permission to be here. We wouldn't have given it, but you need to go, now."

"Fine, but you boys got no idea who you're fucking with," said one of the men.

"Oh, but we do," smiled Hiro. "We're fucking with Los Muertos, run by the sick twisted bastard, Demon. And you all follow him like cows to cud. He beats a girl; you beat a girl. He rapes a girl; you rape a girl. He kills a man; you kill a man. I truly hate men that can't think for themselves."

"Watch yourself, boy," growled the older biker.

"Watch myself? Or what? You're going to do something. Great. Drop the weapons, and let's go, old man. Come on. You want to do something, do it." The man just stood in the middle of the bar, staring at Hiro. He swallowed, looking down at the pistol tucked in his jeans. The other man wasn't even phased by it. "I didn't think so. Cowards never face their enemy head-on."

"You'll be hearin' from Demon," he said.

"I'm very much looking forward to it," smiled Alec.

"Me too," grinned Tailor, slapping his big hands together and rubbing. "I like me some white boy meat."

The four bikers remaining just stared at one another. The one with the knife wound was wrapping his hand in napkins while the other three headed toward the door.

"You taking your buddies with you?" asked Dom.

"You killed 'em; you bury 'em," said the old man. Dom just shook his head, laughing.

"Man, we don't bury anybody. We'll let the gators have a good meal tonight. Oh, and don't worry, we'll make sure their bikes are put to good use." When the four men were gone, Hiro turned to the bartender.

"How long have they been here?"

"Three, maybe four days," he said. "They'd come in every day when I opened and stay till closing time. They were asking for women, but I called my waitresses and told them to stay home. I know those guys; I know what they do to women."

"What did they want?" asked Dom.

"They didn't say. They just kept saying they would wait it out." He looked at the big group of men and shook his head. "You know that they're gonna come back with more men, right? They won't let this slide. You killed their road captain. That's a big role in the organization."

"I know," said Hiro, "but in fairness, he was asking for it."

"Who are you guys?" asked the bartender. Alec stepped up to the bar, his shadow creating a dark void in the room.

"Redemption."

CHAPTER EIGHT

Hiro rushed to his cottage for a quick shower, changed his clothes, and was back out the door knocking on Winter's door at exactly six p.m. He heard the sliding of the locks and chains and smiled to himself. He'd installed not one extra lock but two. Anything to make her feel better.

"You're right on time," she said with a small smile.

"I try to be," he grinned. "Should we sit out here?"

"No," she said, frowning. "It's cold out. We can sit in here." She opened the door wider and waved toward the living room.

"Are you sure, Winter? I don't mind the cold if it will make you feel better," he said.

"I'm sure. Thank you, though. Do you want something to drink?" Hiro shook his head, taking a seat in one of the leather chairs. Looking around the cottage, he noticed that Mama Irene must have come in and done some redecorating. Although the leather chairs were still present, the paintings were of flowers and beautifully colored houses in the Quarter.

"I wanted to thank you again for this afternoon," said Winter. "I'm sure you're not used to women just screaming at the top of their lungs."

"No," he said, giving a small grin, "I'm definitely not, and I'm glad I'm not. I will always be here for you, Winter, always, but it did break my heart to hear you scream like that."

"I know. That tells me exactly what kind of man you are. I had a long chat with Rachelle afterwards, and she explained some things to me that I needed to hear. But first, I promised to tell you more about me. I told you that Demon, the leader, made me touch him when I was a little girl. I was only eight or nine, I think. He would force me to rub him until he…"

"I know, Winter, you don't have to say it," said Hiro.

"He started making me do it out on the floor at night with all the men there. Then he'd make me do them too. I didn't understand it. I didn't know what I was doing. One of the other women, Candy, she tried to protect me, but they just beat her more if she did.

"Before I started my period, she told me what was going to happen and that once that started, Demon was going to start raping me. Candy said I should run. Whenever I got the chance, I should run. I tried. Lots of times, and he always found me."

"He won't find you now, Winter." He was trying to reassure her, or himself. He wasn't quite sure yet.

"That first time, when he raped me," she said, closing her eyes, shaking her head, "he was so brutal, and then he let the other men take turns with me. I was only fourteen. It was Scorch that stopped them. He was an older man, but he said if they continued, they'd kill me. Demon said I was going to be his, and he was going to mark me. He did the very next day. It was more than four years of that before I ran again."

"I'm so sorry, Winter. I wish I could take it all away. I wish I could show you what love is really like for a man and a woman. I know you're terrified and unsure, but I really hope that you'll at least let me be your friend."

"Why would you want someone who is so damaged?" she asked with tears in her eyes. "You could have any woman you wanted. Why me?"

"Because there is something so special about you, Winter. I can't even put my finger on it. I know in my heart that our paths crossed for a reason. We're all damaged, Winter. Every last man and woman here have been damaged in some way. The trick is not to let it kill you. Don't let it steal your joy."

"What if this is all I can give you? I know how relationships are supposed to look. I see it every day here. I watch Keegan and Hawk, the way they hold hands, kiss, and love one another. I see it. I see that he's a good man. It doesn't make him any less scary to me, but I do see it. I see all of the men here with their wives. But what if this, you and me sitting across from one another talking, is all I can give you."

"Is it all you want to give me?" he asked quietly.

"I'm not sure how to answer that," Winter said, standing to walk around the room. "I've never experienced the good, Hiro. How do I know if this is what I want?"

"Only you can answer that, Winter. I know that when I don't see you, I feel empty. I look for you when you're not near me. I like seeing your beautiful face, that gorgeous head of hair. I know that I want more, but I will wait forever if you need it."

Winter grabbed the hairbrush that was lying on the counter and began to brush long strokes through her hair. Carefully, she pulled the hair behind her ears and pulled it into a ponytail. Her fingers touched the tips of her ear, and she stared at Hiro.

"He bit it off," she said quietly. "I wasn't doing something right, and he bit my neck several times, drawing blood, and then bit the tip of my ear off."

"He's an animal," said Hiro, standing from the chair.

"He just spit it out and laughed at me. I have bite marks everywhere, Hiro. How can you possibly look at me, look at those marks, and want to be anywhere near me?"

"They can be fixed, just like the tattoo, if you want." She looked up at him, hope filling her face.

"They can?"

"Yes," he smiled. "Everything can be fixed if you want it fixed."

She turned off the light in the kitchen, standing in the darkness, and walked toward Hiro. He didn't move, didn't dare to breathe in case she decided to run.

"Will you show me what a kind kiss between a man and woman feels like?"

"Are you sure, Winter? I don't want to rush you."

"I'm sure. Just lips, no hands. I've never had a kind kiss."

"Okay," he said, nodding. "I need to get closer."

Winter took a half-step toward him as he did the same. Hiro desperately wanted to touch her skin, to place his hands on her face or shoulders, but he knew that she would panic. Instead, he leaned forward, a breath away from her mouth.

"Softly, I won't hurt you." She nodded, closing her eyes. "Open your eyes, Winter. Look at me. Know that it's me." She opened her eyes as he moved toward her. His warm lips touched hers, just settling against the flesh for a brief moment. There was nothing violent, nothing forceful. It was just a soft, sweet, gentle kiss.

Hiro pulled back and stared down at her face. She looked at him and nodded.

"Okay."

"Okay?" he asked, grinning. "What does that mean?"

"It means, it was okay. I wasn't scared. Can we eat now?" Hiro laughed, nodding his head.

"Yes, we can eat now."

CHAPTER NINE

Hiro smiled at the heaping mound of food on Winter's plate. Usually, she would eat small portions of food, but tonight, she seemed exceptionally hungry or perhaps more comfortable in her surroundings. Hiro didn't care which it was. He was just happy she was eating more.

"Are you trying to compete with Brit?" smiled Aiden. At first, he worried that Winter might be embarrassed and run, but instead, she gave him the smallest of smiles and nodded.

"I think I should try to keep up," she said. Aiden laughed, trying to keep his tone low. Winter looked at the people at the table. Hiro was to her left, and Keegan and Hawk were on her right. Also at their table were Eagle, Tinley, Brit, Aiden, and Dom.

"I didn't get regular meals," she said quietly. "Demon, the man that owned me..."

"He didn't own you," said Hiro. "No one can own another human. No one." She nodded.

"He would let me have small amounts of food. I think he thought that if he kept me hungry, I couldn't run. Candy, this other woman that was there, she would come down at night when I was in the cage and toss me up bread or biscuits. Until I came here, I never realized how wonderful food could be."

"I'm sure George and Mama Irene would be happy to hear that," smiled Tinley. "You've changed these last few days, Winter. It's nice to see you being more open and joining us for our meals."

"I owe you all an apology," she said, staring at the table. "I should have been more grateful to you for giving me this chance. I especially owe all of you, the men, an apology. I wish I could change. I'm trying, but it will take some time."

"You have all the time in the world," said Hiro.

"I know you think that, but what if Demon and the others come for me? I need to be stronger than I am now. I need to not be so terrified that I just fall down and allow them to take me again."

"May I suggest something?" said the deep baritone voice. To her credit, Winter didn't jump. She stared at the dark man, his long black hair, shiny and silky. His eyes were like pools of dark chocolate, but they weren't menacing. They were kind. Running between his legs were two little boys.

"Are they yours?" she asked quietly.

"They are my grandsons," he said, smiling. It was uncharacteristic for Trak, but when speaking of his family, he almost always smiled. "JB? Tobias? Say hello to Winter."

"Hello," said JB, shyly standing behind his grandfather's legs.

"Hi," smiled Tobias. "Isn't winter a time of year?" She nodded at the little boy.

"It is, but it's also a name," she said. "I chose it for myself."

"You were saying you had a suggestion, Trak?" asked Hiro.

"Yes. I think when she is ready, Winter will benefit from some self-defense classes, including the use of a knife or gun." The young woman started to protest, but Trak held up his hand. "I'm not suggesting that you harm anyone, but it's nice to know that you have the ability if you're ever in a bad situation. Almost all of the women here have gone through some sort of training, including my wife and daughters. If you don't wish to learn from me or Hiro, we can ask Piper or Ani to teach you."

"Can I think about it?" she asked.

"Yes." That was all he said, turning to head back toward Lauren and the others. His grandsons were still clinging to his legs, and he was walking as if he didn't even know they were there.

"He's sort of scary, but not," said Winter.

"Trak is a very well-trained man," said Eagle. "He was with Delta. Do you know what that is?" Winter shook her head, staring at the others.

"I mentioned once before that all of the men here are former Special Forces in the military," said Hawk. "Eagle and I served in the Marine Corps as snipers. Aiden was an Army Ranger. Dom was MARSOC, special forces for the Marines. We have men who were Navy SEALs, Coast Guard, just about everything."

"And you're all trained differently than regular military men and women?" she asked.

"Yes," smiled Hiro. "I was regular Army, but I've been trained in a dozen different forms of martial arts. It made me desirable for my team. The others, they've all been trained in ways none of us can imagine."

"So, how is Delta different?" she asked.

"It's not so much that Delta is different. It's that Trak is different," said Hawk. "There are some men born to be warriors, Winter."

"And some born to be demons?" she asked.

"Yes, honey, I'm afraid so. Trak was born to be a warrior. To save others, even if it meant sacrificing himself. He's unlike anyone here, and even as a grandfather, his skills are still what we all strive for. I can tell you that I've watched a lot of men come through here, and Hiro is right up there at the top."

"You don't have to say that," said Hiro, shaking his head. "I'm as good as any of you, except Trak." He grinned.

"You're better, Hiro. You just don't know it," said Aiden. He grabbed Brit's hand, headed to the desserts.

"Good evenin'," said Mama Irene. "Is my boat gonna be ready for Mardi Gras?"

"Oh, yes," said Winter, clearing her throat. "I also wanted to thank you for screaming with me today. It was wonderful."

"We girls gotta stick together," smiled Irene. "Sometimes, you just gotta let it go. Believe me, Matthew knows that I need a good yell now and then." Gabi came up to stand by Irene, smiling at the table.

"How are you feeling, Winter?"

"Um, okay, I guess. I was wondering. Hiro said you might be able to remove the bite marks on me." She asked it so casually, the table almost didn't hear it. Keegan looked down at her lap, hoping Winter wouldn't see her tears. Gabi stared at her for a moment, then nodded.

"Yes, I think we can help with that, but I have a suggestion for Hiro first. The pond."

"The pond?" he said, staring at Gabi. "I totally forgot about that. The pond might be able to help. Can you swim?"

"No," she said, shaking her head. "I've never been in any water except a shower or tub."

"If you'll give me your trust, Winter, I won't break it. I promise. But it will require full trust on your part."

"You won't hurt me, right?"

"Never."

"Okay, I trust you," she said, standing. Hiro didn't reach for her hand. He just stood beside her, waiting for her to walk toward the door. "Should I hold your hand?"

"If you want to, I'd like that a lot," he said, smiling. Clumsily, she reached for his hand, trying to wrap her fingers with his. Hiro wanted to laugh, but there was truly nothing funny about it. Every child from pre-school on learned how to hold hands.

"Let's try this," he said, taking her hand. He laid her palm flat against his, folding his fingers over the back of her hand. "There. Now you don't feel trapped by my fingers, and you can let go any time you want. Okay?" She nodded.

"It feels strange to touch someone's hand like this. Your hands are bigger than I thought. A lot bigger than mine." Winter could feel the panic rising in her chest and looked down at their hands once more. He wasn't coming closer. He wasn't squeezing her hand. He wasn't doing anything except allowing her hand to rest in his.

"Ready?" She nodded as they walked out the door and toward the pond. Rachelle stood in the middle of the cafeteria, waving her hands up and down to quiet the room. When they were gone from sight, out of range of the noise, she raised her hands.

"Hiro the hero!" There were loud cheers and clapping as everyone felt a collective sigh of relief.

"Is she on her way, Rach?" asked Mac.

"We can hope. What I can tell you all is that is the first time I've seen her make human contact other than this afternoon crying and screaming. It's as if it opened the door for her. Hiro is truly a miracle worker."

"Where are we going?" she asked as they walked the well-lit path.

"Belle Fleur, this house and land, has secrets that none of us understand. It's ancient and wonderful and beautiful. A few years ago, it was discovered that there is a pond on the property that has certain mineral elements in it. It helps to keep everyone young."

"You drink it?"

"No," he grinned. "You swim in it. The water helps to heal wounds, scars, aches, pains. Mama Irene and Matthew are in their nineties, but they move and look as though they're in their sixties."

"I guess I didn't put the math together," she said, shaking her head. "So, you think the pond will take away the bite marks?"

"Maybe. It's a worth a try, isn't it?"

"But I can't swim," she said as they walked down the dock.

"This is where I need you to trust me, Winter. We're both going to have to get naked." Her eyes went wide with fear, and Hiro cursed himself. "I won't touch you, not in that way. I'll only hold your hands so that you can stay afloat in the water. It's very warm, like bathwater. I promise, Winter."

"You won't touch me down there?" she asked, staring at him.

"No, honey. I won't touch you down there. I swear to you." She nodded, and he turned toward the water. "Why don't you turn around, and I'll go in first. I have to undress, so I'll be naked as well, but when you turn around, I'll be in the water. You won't see me."

Winter nervously turned her back on Hiro. She heard the sounds of him undressing, and a panic rose inside her. As frightened as she was, she remained still, just waiting. The sound of water from behind her made her turn. Hiro's dark head was wet as he looked up at Winter, smiling.

"I'll turn around, okay?" She nodded as he turned in the water, facing the waterfall at the back of the pond. Carefully folding her clothes, she stood in the cold wind and looked down at her body. Sitting on the edge of the dock, she dangled her feet in the warm water.

"What do I do now? I can't swim."

"This will be hard, Winter, but I'm going to have to turn and grab your hands so you don't drown. I won't touch your body, just your hands, okay?"

"Okay."

Hiro turned, seeing her petite body sitting quietly, shivering on the edge of the dock. He reached for her hands, and she leaned into his, falling into the water. When her head went under, her face and hair soaked, she panicked and reached for him. Wrapping her arms around his neck, she practically climbed his body, trying to hold on.

"Whoa, whoa, honey, it's okay," he said calmly. Hiro wasn't even sure where to put his hands. He didn't need to hold her since she was holding on so tightly to him. "Winter, I need to put my hands at your waist, and I need, I don't want it, but I need for you to unwind your legs from around my body."

"I c-can't," she said, staring at him.

"I don't want to frighten you, Winter, but your body being close to mine is making me react physically to you. I won't do anything, but you're going to feel it if you move just a millimeter." She stared at his face, relaxing the hold around his body. Her bottom touched the tip of his cock, and for just a moment, a sense of panic rose in her throat.

This wasn't Demon. This wasn't the sweaty, disgusting men at Los Muertos. This was Hiro. His cock was hard like theirs, but he wasn't shoving it at her. He was trying to be kind. Loosening her grip around his neck, he let out a long sigh, pushing her further away from his body. The warm water didn't help his situation, but at least she wouldn't feel threatened.

"Keep your hands locked around my neck and just gently kick your feet back and forth. You won't drown. I won't let you."

"What do I need to do? I mean, in the pond."

"Nothing," he smiled. "Just enjoy the warm waters and relax. They'll do what they were meant to do." She nodded, staring at Hiro.

"You didn't say anything," she said, looking down at her body.

"It's not my business," said Hiro. "I think you're beautiful whether you're a brunette or blonde, but it's up to you."

"My hair color always gave me away," she said. "About a year ago, I realized that I could dye it. Red was too noticeable, and black seemed extreme for me, so I chose this brown. No one sees the other." Hiro tried to control his smile. He saw it. It was the first thing that caught his eye while she sat on that dock. A big fluff of blonde hair. All natural.

"There are other things you can do, for down there," he said, clearing his throat. "You should ask Keegan, but you can wax or shave."

"I know," she said, nodding. "I guess I didn't think it mattered since no one was seeing it. I haven't had a man touch me in more than five years, Hiro. This is very strange for me. When I was staying at the women's shelter, the director made sure that I was checked for diseases. I didn't even know you could get diseases from that." Her head nodded downward toward his cock.

"Yes, unfortunately, you can," he said. "In the military, men are tested every six months to be sure they haven't contracted something. If they're smart, they use condoms to protect themselves and common sense. Not everyone does. Here we're asked to do the same."

"I was lucky," she said. "I had an infection, but it was cleared with medication. Gabi and Riley said it was cleared up as well."

"Winter? Why are you telling me this?" asked Hiro.

"Because – because one day, I think I might like for you to touch me there," she said, staring at him. "Candy, the woman at the club, she said that when you really like a man, you get warm down there, and your stomach feels as though it has butterflies in it. I thought I was just scared when I saw you, but I think now it might be that I like you."

"I like you, too, Winter," he said, smiling. "I'm glad you feel that way." His hands were still at her waist, holding her straight out so their bodies wouldn't touch.

"The wind is cold," she said, shivering. "I think I might like for you to hold me closer."

Hiro gave a small head jerk and slowly moved her body closer to his own. She felt the stiff, rigid mass against her stomach, and for a moment, the terror and panic bubbled up in her, then just as quickly, it died down. Hiro just held her against his chest, her arms now hanging freely around his neck.

"Is this what it's supposed to be like? Are you supposed to feel warmth and safety?"

"Yea, honey, that's exactly what you should feel."

"Will you kiss me again?" she asked.

"I will, but just so you know, you can always kiss me any time you want. You don't even have to ask me."

"Never?"

"Never," he smiled.

Winter leaned forward, pressing her lips hard against his own. He didn't fight her. He didn't try to tell her she was doing it wrong. He let her explore in her way and in her own time. Turning her head slightly, her lips parted to force his upper lip between her own. Hiro was about to explode. She turned her head again, then relaxed, kissing him, and pulling away, then kissing him again.

"Was that better than okay?" he grinned.

"Yes," she smiled. "Candy said that sometimes men like to stick their tongues in your mouth."

"Did the men never do that?" asked Hiro.

"No," she said, shaking her head. "They didn't kiss at all." For some reason, that made Hiro very happy. It was as if something had been left of her innocence.

"She's right. When a man and woman truly care for one another, using your tongues during a kiss can be extremely intimate and exciting."

Winter seemed to be contemplating that idea when she looked down in the water, seeing Hiro's cock. She always hated that word, but it was the only thing she knew to call it other than penis, and that word seemed too juvenile. Where the other men's penises always looked disgusting, his was beautiful. It was long and thick but didn't look painful. There was dark hair surrounding the pale skin, his stomach muscles rolling with every kick of his legs and breath of his body.

"You can touch me if you like, Winter. I won't touch you back unless you want me to, but I don't care if you're curious."

Instinctively she reached into the water and touched the velvety soft skin. It was vastly different from Demon. Everything about it seemed good, not evil. How was that possible? Looking at Hiro, his eyes were closed, and she realized how difficult this was for him. Releasing him, she wrapped her arms around his neck again and lay her lips to his.

"Thank you, Hiro. Thank you for bringing me here," she whispered.

"My pleasure. Shall we see if it's worked?" he asked.

Nodding, she held onto him as he swam toward the dock and easily lifted her out of the water. She shivered as he grabbed a towel from the wooden towel bin and wrapped her up. Looking down, she gasped.

"They're gone," she said, looking at her stomach. "I can't believe it! They're gone!"

"Turn," he said, smiling. She turned, and he lifted her hair. The bite marks on her neck were gone. She touched the tip of her ear and frowned. "It can't make flesh grow back. But it appears all the scars are gone, even the lash marks on your back."

"I can't believe this," she said, shaking her head. "With my dark hair, the scars and tattoo gone, he might not even know me."

"Let's not risk it, okay. For now, stay on-property." He rubbed the towel over his body and quickly dressed. When he was done, he turned his back so that Winter could do the same. Finished, he walked her to her cottage, kissed her sweetly, and then heard the locks engage.

Looking down at his erect cock he frowned. This was going to be a true test of his patience.

Damn.

CHAPTER TEN

"Where's Ratchet?" growled Demon.

The woman kneeling in front of him was going to town on his dick, but she wasn't doing it fast enough. He leaned forward, slapping her bare ass with the belt in his hand. She cried out and continued sucking and stroking. Her blonde hair wasn't quite as blonde as Girl's, but it was pretty enough. He loved blondes. True, natural blondes.

"Dead," said the old man.

"How?" he asked casually.

"Chinaman killed him. Squeezed his throat so hard it killed him."

"One Chinaman killed Ratchet?" he scoffed. "Stupid bastard. Where?"

"We were near New Orleans, trying to track down Girl. Someone said they thought she was in the area, but this other club said we were on their property. Killed Rat and Tug, too. Fed 'em to the gators."

"Where's their bikes?" asked Demon, gripping the woman's head and holding her down. She gagged, the sound only exciting him more.

"They took 'em," said the old man.

Demon let out a roar of relief as he spewed cum all over the woman's face. Her makeup was smeared everywhere, and he wanted to kill her in that moment. Instead, he jerked his head to two other men standing nearby.

"Have fun, boys. She's all yours," he said.

"No," she whispered. "Please, I did what you asked, please." She saw it coming but couldn't move fast enough. He swung the belt at her, the red welts rising against her soft, white skin. The buckle hit her buttocks, and blood oozed from the open wound.

Another man grabbed her by the waist, yanking her toward the pool tables as she kicked and screamed, crying, begging for someone to help her.

"Don't worry, girly," said Spit, "I'm only gonna fuck your ass. My boy, Ripe can have your pussy."

The cries and screams didn't even bother Demon as he stood and zipped his jeans. He couldn't remember the last time he showered but knew it had been a while. The stench was getting to him as well.

"What's their club called?" he asked.

"Don't know. They weren't wearing kuttes, but there were some big bastards in the group, Demon. Bigger than Tug, way bigger. The little Chinaman, he knew all that fancy kung fu shit. Never even pulled a weapon."

"Find out who they are," he growled. "And someone fucking find me Girl."

CHAPTER ELEVEN

Winter stared at the room full of women who were laughing and joking. It wasn't her first time attending one of the 'wellness' meetings, but she was still amazed that they could all be so happy, so filled with joy, in spite of the things they'd endured. She wanted to be like them. She wanted to let go of her past and move forward, and she was pretty sure that would be with Hiro.

In true George and Mama Irene fashion, cookies and brownies of various flavors were lying on pretty plates while coffee, tea, and hot chocolate filled their cups. George had even set out a glass filled with peppermint sticks and marshmallows, just for Winter.

"I wanted to smack him; he was so damn handsome," smiled Tinley. "God, that man, he looked at me, and I knew I was in trouble. As terrified as I was, he still got me to go to bed with him and then got me pregnant with triplets! Triplets, for God's sake!"

"Aren't you happy about that?" asked Winter as she looked at the women laughing.

"Now, yes. Very, very happy, but you have to remember I was a woman in my forties, so my pregnancy was risky. Plus, multiples are always riskier. Now, Ty, little Hawk, and Benji are my whole world. Although, I can hardly call them little any longer since they're all bigger than me."

"Did he make you have sex with him?" Winter asked with a confused expression.

"No, honey, he didn't. He asked me; he wooed me; he made me feel things I hadn't felt ever in my entire life. That's why I had sex with him. I continued to have sex with him, make love to him because he is a good, kind, wonderful man who loves me."

"Winter? Did anyone ever explain what true sex in relationships should look like and feel like?" asked Rachelle.

"Candy, the only woman that ever tried to help me, she tried to explain. I don't think she really knew either. Her father was one of the bikers, so they didn't abuse her the way they did me, but she still had to do things. She was right about the feeling, though. You know, the one you get inside when you really like someone. I feel that when I'm around Hiro. I get warm on the inside, and I feel like I want to touch him."

"I see," smiled Rachelle. "Did you tell Hiro this?"

"Yes, the other night at the pond. He promised he wouldn't touch me, and he didn't, but then I wanted him to touch me. It was like I needed him to touch me, but I was still so scared, and he knew it. He knew I was frightened and was trying so hard to help me. No one other than Candy has ever helped me.

"He let me touch him, anywhere I wanted to, but he didn't make me do anything. I didn't have to rub him or open my legs or anything. It was really strange because I didn't get scared or sick when I touched him. I just got really warm all over."

"Oh, sweet girl, I'm so sorry you had those terrible experiences," said Marie. "Winter, sex with a man, lovemaking is a wonderous experience. Mama always described it as euphoria, a feeling of floating above the clouds. The emotions are raw and terrifying but unlike anything you've ever felt before. You should never feel frightened or concerned for your well-being. A man, a true man, knows that you touch a woman gently and with kindness and respect."

"Do you just open your legs when they ask?"

"Wow, we really do have to start at the beginning, don't we?" smiled Rachelle. "No, sweetie, a lady doesn't just open her legs when a man asks. First of all, he would never just say, 'open your legs,' he might ask you to open your legs wider if you're making love, but it wouldn't be crude. If you care for the other person and you're in bed, loving one another, he's going to ask permission for everything he does, especially the first time you're together. After that, he may not ask permission because you have a relationship. You're familiar with one another. If you don't want to do something, then you don't."

"I don't think I've ever been touched in bed," she said quietly. Several of the women had to look away, hiding the tears that filled their eyes. "If you refuse, he won't hit you?" she asked the room.

"Never," said Lauren. "In my thirty-plus years of marriage to Trak, he has never raised a hand at me. Never. But I can also tell you that I love him so much, I've never refused him. I want him to touch me. That's the difference, Winter."

"Same." A chorus of women agreed.

"Then why? Why would these men hurt women, hurt me? There were dozens over the years. It wasn't just me. What did I do to them? I'm not big enough to hurt them. I'm not strong or powerful. Why?"

"Because they're broken," said Mama Irene, walking towards her. "Men like that are broken inside, honey. Their own mamas or daddies hurt 'em, or someone did. It's not anything you did. You were a baby when you came into their world. You did nothing to deserve what they did to you. All you can do now is move on, live your life."

"How did you all do it?" she asked, looking at the faces.

"Gaspar," smiled Alexandra. "He made me forget every horrible thing that man did to me by touching me in a way that only a gentle man knows how to do. Even when I couldn't have children of my own, I still ended up with six of the most beautiful creatures on this earth because of him."

"Same," said Sophia. "Ivan is my hero in every way. We have five beautiful children because of his generosity and kindness. I love him so much I can't even begin to describe it. My world wasn't quite like yours, Winter, but it was a hell of its own kind. Ivan saved me from that."

"It seems odd that it was men that hurt us and men that rescued us," said Winter. "Are women the same? Are there evil women and good women?"

"Yes," said Rose. "It was a woman that tried to kill Alec and Mac. In fact, she was a high-ranking official in the government. She killed many men before they found out who she was."

"It was also, technically, a woman that hurt Trevor," said Ashley. "She had a sex change, but when he knew her, she was a woman. She killed several men before being caught."

"Once I learned to read, I read anything that I could get my hands on. While I was running, some days, I would just find a library and sit inside all day, reading any book I could find. I found out that the childhood I had was not normal. I read about parents who gave their children bubble baths and read stories to them, cooked for them, and played outside with them. I watched movies about happy families, and I tried to understand why I didn't have that.

"The director at the shelter said I was one of the lost. No one knew who I was or where I came from. No one cared. I was just lost. All alone."

"You're not all alone now," smiled Cait. "Now, you have all of us, and you have a man who cares for you, watches out for you."

"Watches out for me?" she asked, looking puzzled.

"Honey, he's been sitting on that bench out there near the gardens the whole time we've been in here. He paid for the laser to remove your tattoo. He installed your extra locks. He made sure your favorite foods were always available. He put the jelly beans in your cottage." She turned to see Hiro pacing in front of the bench.

"He watches out for me," she said with tears in her eyes. "He watches out for me."

"He watches out for you, baby," said Mama Irene. "He makes sure that no one hurts you, no one comes near you unless you want it. That's a special kind of man."

"I don't know what to do." She looked at Hiro, then back at all of the other women. There was excitement in her eyes but also fear.

"What do you want to do?" asked Alexandra.

"I want to hug him, like he hugged me the other day and made me feel better, made me know I was cared for. I want to do that for him."

"Then go do it," said Mama Irene, smiling at her. Running from the cafeteria, she didn't even grab her coat. Irene smiled at the other women and stood, leaving them to their therapy session.

"She's going to be okay," said Rachelle, looking at Ashley.

"I do believe she is."

Hiro paced in front of the stone bench, waiting patiently, or not so patiently, for Winter to come out of the therapy session with the other women. He could see her brown ponytail bobbing up and down, but he couldn't see her face. He desperately wanted to protect her from the world, but especially from the world of Los Muertos. He wasn't going to allow them to ever touch her again.

She was everything he wanted, and he didn't even know why. When she was around him, he felt complete; he felt whole and at home. Looking up, he saw her open the cafeteria door and start running toward him. At first, he worried that she'd uncovered something in her past and was crying. Instead, she was smiling, running straight for him.

Bracing himself, he reached for her as she launched herself into his arms, wrapping herself around his body, kissing the side of his face.

"Oh, wow," he said against her neck, tears coming to his eyes.

"I wanted to hug you," she said, sniffling back a tear. "I wanted to hug you and make you feel the way I felt when you hugged me. Did it work?"

"Well," he laughed, "why don't you tell me what you felt when I hugged you?"

"I felt warm and safe and happy. It was as if something switched on inside me and the huge sadness was less than before. I didn't feel alone any longer, and I wasn't as scared as I once was."

"That's exactly what I'm feeling, Winter," he said, kissing her forehead. "Exactly."

"I think I know you won't hurt me, not ever. I don't think any of these men will hurt me, will they?" she asked with a smile.

"No, baby, none of these men will ever hurt you, and I definitely will not. It might take a while to get used to the loud noises and the dogs, even the men who sometimes look like they're angry, but they aren't. But we'll get through this together, you and I. We'll continue with therapy, we'll make sure that you get comfortable with everyone, and we can even bring the dogs around more if you think that might help. They're great companions and protectors."

"Okay."

"Okay?" he asked, laughing.

"Yes. Now, I'm hungry."

CHAPTER TWELVE

Hiro walked with the others to the auditorium for their morning meeting. Los Muertos was the hot topic of the day and where they were. He noticed a new face in the group, then realized that it was someone he recognized.

"Thomas? Is that you?" he asked, smiling at the man.

"It's me," he said, nodding. He pulled the man in for a hug, slapping his back.

"I almost didn't recognize you. You look amazing! Are you working out now?" asked Hiro.

"Yes, the rehab center that Ryan recommended focuses on not just getting patients drug-free but also getting your mind and body right. It was something I'd ignored for too long, believing that my brain would carry me through any situation. Perhaps had I been more physically fit, I could have fought off Stevens and his men."

"Don't think like that," said Hiro, shaking his head. "You did what you needed to do in the moment. All that matters now is that you're healing and on the right path. Are you joining us permanently?"

"I am," he smiled. "I never thought I would find my way back to the people I thought of as family, but here I am."

"Can I ask how old you are? I mean, you're some super scientist genius who's done all this amazing shit, but you don't look old enough."

"Well, thank you, and yes, I suppose I don't really look old enough. I'm thirty-three."

"Damn, I really need to read a few more books," smiled Hiro.

"Don't be modest, Hiro. I know that you have an exceptionally high IQ, and you hide it from everyone else." Hiro said nothing, his expression not giving anything away. Thomas smiled at the other man. "Alright, I'll keep that under wraps for now."

"Okay, everyone, take a seat," said Luke. "We've got the Los Muertos to talk about."

"Souls of the dead," said Jax. "I wonder if those are good souls or evil souls."

"I think we know the answer to that," smirked Cruz.

"I think we're certain of that," said Cam. "Tech boys have done an amazing job pulling data on these guys, and it wasn't fucking easy. Code?" The men from the tech team walked down the steps and made their way to the front of the room.

"Some of what you're about to see is going to haunt you, but you need to see it," said Ace. "These assholes were dumb enough to post shit for their members, photos, texts, all kinds of crap out there on the web. Hiro, no one will think badly of you if you want to leave."

"No," he said resolutely. Code gave him a quick nod and took control of the floor.

"Demon, or Warren Joseph Bell, Jr., is currently the head of the Los Muertos. His father, Sr., was ready to take over about thirty years ago when Jr. decided he was better suited for the job. When the grandfather kicked the bucket, he killed his old man.

"Up until then, the Los Muertos was like any other one-percenter club. They weren't exactly legitimate and on the up-and-up, but they didn't murder without provocation or rape women. They had the usual club whores, that sort of thing, dabbled in a little drug selling, but nothing horrible. Until Jr.

"He came in and made it very clear that every man would be required to do certain things. Usually, when a new leader takes over, men are offered the opportunity to leave. Not Los Muertos. If you wanted to leave, you had to fight your way out of a gauntlet. Two rows of men with bats, chains, you name it, and if you made it to the end, you were home free. Only one made it. His injuries were so severe he was hospitalized for almost a year. He was never the same after that and ended up dying of lung cancer two years ago.

"Demon believes that he has the ultimate say in everyone's life. They're dealing in drugs and women. The more abused, the more addicted, the better. These women are not going to some sheik for his private harem. These women are being sent to some of the worst brothels and whorehouses in the world. They're hooked on drugs, beaten daily, starved, and used in every unimaginable way." Code nodded toward Ace, who took over.

"Demon doesn't want the men to have wives or girlfriends. If they choose to have one, the stipulation is that he gets to use them whenever he wants. These are some of the photos that were passed from one man to the next. They are graphic," said Ace. "More graphic than anything we've ever shown."

"Commonplace for them is taking a new girl and tying her to a pool table in the common room. They rape her while beating her, sodomize her, force her to have oral sex, and more. All with at least ten men, usually more. Some of these girls aren't even teenagers yet. This photo," he said, looking up at Hiro's face, "this photo was taken about ten years ago. In the cage above the floor is Winter, naked, terrified, and alone. She looks like she might be ten years old, but from the date, we know she's older."

"I'm going to kill him," said Hiro. Luke looked at the man, concerned for his mental state.

"We're going to kill them all," said Cam. "This isn't a mission where we go in and save them. We're going to go in and wipe them out. The feds have a folder on these guys that's ten inches thick, but they've yet to send anyone to finish them off. We're going to do our civic duty and do so." Ace continued.

"Five nights ago, four girls, all only twelve, were taken from a birthday party at an amusement park. The cameras have them being thrown into a van, and it drove away. One of the girls suffers from seizures and has a bracelet that sends signals to her parents. They reported it to the police, but no one went out to try and find her, so the parents took it upon themselves."

"Oh, fuck," muttered Eli.

"Yea, oh fuck. The father was killed, shot in the head, and dumped on the side of the road. The mother is still there from what we know. They had five clubhouses as of two years ago. Now they only have two. One in Nevada and one in Arizona. One of them that was closed was located in Colorado. They sold the property to a real estate investment group. Cash. When they began the demolition of the buildings, they discovered some rather gruesome things.

"One was an underground bunker with cages and a wide variety of what can only be described as torture devices. The other was a mass grave with as many as twenty women and thirty babies. We've petitioned the courts to have access to the other sites that are still up for sale."

"All this and the feds still haven't stepped in?" asked Hiro.

"No, and here's why. They claim that Demon is working with them on bringing down a major crime family in Yugoslavia that's been bringing in drugs and women to the states for years."

"Is that a fucking joke?" said Luke.

"I wish it were," said Ace. "I tried to tell them that this man isn't capable of doing any such thing, and they said he's given them great evidence so far. I don't believe it, but we've got Bodwick helping us to track down the information on the federal end."

"The brutality of these attacks," started Sly. He looked at the room and swallowed, shaking his head. "We've seen a lot of shit in our time together. A lot. The autopsy reports on the bodies in the pit were horrendous. It was so brutal. These women suffered dislocated hips, knees, and shoulders. Two had pelvic fractures that were most likely caused from men leaning on their pelvic bones as they raped them. Their faces would have been unrecognizable had they survived. These men don't deserve to live. None of them, and I've never said that before."

Cam, Luke, and Eric looked toward their fathers, the seniors. The dark clouds over their faces told them everything they needed to know. This was going to be an assassination squad.

"Los Muertos is hiding out right now," said Ace. "We know they have facilities in Arizona, and that's where we believe they are. The problem is we're not certain where. The girls that disappeared were from Colorado. I trolled the web for most of the night, looking for anything that might help us. Demon posted a picture of the four girls, all naked, tied to a pole in what appears to be a basement.

"Their faces… the terror on their faces is more than I can stand to see. We know that the old man from the bar went back with the others and told his story because Demon called out to other clubs for any help. So far, no one has taken him up on his request. They're planning to come here; we just don't know how many yet."

"We'll be ready for them," said Cam. "I will not allow that filth in my state, let alone near our compound."

"Skull, Tango, and Razor have been working on the bikes non-stop with the help of Ryan. We're equipping them with some surprises."

"Oh, man," smiled Axel, "do I smell superhero motorcycle?"

"Something like that," smiled Skull. "They'll have weapons capabilities that can only be fired with retinal identifiers, holsters for larger weapons, and small rocket launchers. They won't have a clue what hit them if we have to face them on the bikes."

"Axel? Eli? I know your clubs weren't quite like this, but any insights you can give us would be helpful," said Luke.

"I've been away from that a long time, brother," said Eli. "My father was one of the worst. I saw him beat and rape women, only to see them come back for more. It was a game. They enjoyed hanging at the clubhouse and getting drunk or high. The difference is they were offered protection and food and clothing. If they wanted to leave, they could. When I took over, it was banned. Girls could hang for protection or a home, but no one was abused on my watch."

"Same for me," said Axel. "My old man was brutal. I left before any of that touched me, but it's a lifestyle none of you can understand. These guys are dirty in every way. They could give a shit if they smell or shower. They fight dirty. They fuck dirty. It's not something you guys can relate to because you're different men."

"I will give one piece of advice," said Eli, "make sure that when this starts, the women are in the Sugar Lodge with protection. Lots of protection."

"We're going to need every man here to take them down," said Luke.

"I'll call Fitch and Bron," said Frank. "They're both nearing retirement and were able to help us before. If we can get them here along with some of the cousins, we should be okay."

"We've also got the new security fencing," said Ryan, smiling. "Everything is electric. Even if they cut the power, there is a backup solar power system that will run it for days. But my suggestion is that we meet them where they are, not where we are."

"Hiro? You have to let Winter know," said Cam. "She's going to fucking flip out if you don't. Find a way to let her know that she's safe here."

"Wait! Wait a minute!" said Ally, coming into the auditorium.

"Ally, baby, are you okay?" asked Vince.

"I'm good, sorry. I didn't mean to scare you." She leaned forward, catching her breath. "Listen, some of you know that I was once in a club, involuntarily. Bad mistake as a teenager, got away, moving on. I contacted a few people I knew that were still in that lifestyle. Demon doesn't just want Winter back; he wants her to belong to him. In their world, that means his wife."

"His wife? Fucking no," said Hiro.

"I know, Hiro, but that's what he wants. In fact, he doesn't even know her by that name. They all just call her Girl. My contact said they called their club president and said he was searching for a woman with light blonde hair and brown eyes."

"But..." started Eric.

"I was in on her physicals," said Ally, "she's a natural blonde."

"Keep her hair brown," said Luke. "See if she'll let Keegan cut it, make it look different somehow. We have to make sure he can't get to her."

"We can do that," said Hiro.

"How, wise one?" smirked Cam.

"Easy. There's going to be a wedding this afternoon."

CHAPTER THIRTEEN

"Hiro! Hiro, fucking stop!" yelled Cam as he started toward the door.

"You won't change my mind on this, Cam. It's one way I can protect her. If she becomes Mrs. Tanaka, he'll have a hard time figuring out that it's her. I can watch over her and make sure she survives until we kill that bastard."

"Hiro, honey, she may never be able to have a normal life with you," said Ally sympathetically. "Have you really thought about this?"

The eyes of a hundred men stared at him. Hiro had thought about it. He wanted a life with a wife, a home, and children. He wanted a dog and a picket fence, but he wanted Winter more.

"I've thought about it," he said. "This is my decision. My choice."

"I get it," smirked Pigsty.

"You would," said Nine, nudging his friend.

"Sweetie, she may not be okay with this," said Ally, gripping his arm.

"I know that," he said, nodding, "don't you think I know that. I'll have to try and convince her it's the best option. I'm not sure she even fully understands it, but I swear to you all, I won't hurt her."

"Brother," said Ben, walking toward him, "we know that. Fuck, Hiro, of all of us, I think you're the least likely to hurt her. You're a good man, brother. The best. I know you won't hurt her or do anything that she isn't ready for, but she may not understand what getting married entails."

"Ally?" Cam looked toward their friend. "Would you see if she'll join us? I think we need to have a conversation. I'll call Ashley and Rachelle to get them down here as well."

"Sure, Cam. I'll go find her."

"No, I'll do it," said Hiro. "She needs to hear this from me first."

Hiro left the auditorium, the eyes boring into his back. Ally looked at Vince, wringing her hands in front of her. He gave her a sympathetic look and then patted the seat next to him.

"I'm sorry I didn't tell you I was calling my friend," she said, hugging him.

"You don't have to tell me every move you make, Ally. We're not that kind of couple. I'm glad you did it. It gives us insight into what might be happening."

"Now we just have to hope that she sees it the same way."

Hiro spotted Winter sitting in her favorite spot alongside the maze. The stone bench seemed to give her comfort, often spending hours just sitting there by herself. When she saw him walking toward her, she smiled.

He felt the pit form in his stomach. That smile might be short-lived when he tells her what she needs to know.

"Hi," she said, standing. She wrapped her arms around his waist and hugged him. She was so small her head barely hit his sternum.

"I love your hugs," he grinned.

"Me too. I mean, I love your hugs," she smiled. "You look sad."

"I'm not sad, but I do need to tell you something. The rest of the team is waiting for us in the auditorium." She nodded, staring at him. "Did you know that Demon wanted you as his, as his wife?"

"He always said I belonged to him, but he never said wife. That's different, right?"

"Yes, honey, that's very different. But I think in his world, they are one and the same. Ally knows someone that is familiar with the Los Muertos. He has been asking around about you again and wants you as his."

"I knew he would," she said calmly. "Do I need to leave?"

"What?" Hiro's shocked expression made her feel better. "No, absolutely not. In fact, everyone wants to speak with you, but I think I have a plan that will keep you safe, Winter."

"You do?"

"I do, but you might not like it."

"If you're trying to keep me safe, I think I'll like it, Hiro," she smiled.

"Alright, that's a good start. I think a way to keep you safe is to marry you, Winter." She stared at him, a confused expression covering her face. She tilted her head to the right then the left.

"Marry me? But don't you have to love me to marry me? You'll want to sleep in my bed."

"Love helps, Winter. I won't lie about that. I like you a lot, maybe even love you," he smiled. "I won't sleep in your bed unless you want me to. For now, we can even stay in our own cottages. What this will do for you is give another layer of protection. You will become Mrs. Hirohito Tanaka. He would never suspect that it's you. The others even thought cutting your hair might be a good idea."

Winter walked around him, circling his body. Hiro remained quiet and still, watching her think over his proposition.

"You wouldn't make me have sex with you?" He shook his head. "But if we're married, aren't I supposed to do that?" Hiro gave a tiny smirk.

"Winter, I won't make you do anything that you're not ready for. One day, when you're comfortable with me and maybe even love me a little, we can talk about it. I'm okay with nothing happening right now."

"Are you going to divorce me when he's dead?"

"I-I don't want to," he said with a surprised tone. "I haven't thought about it, but the idea of divorcing you is not appealing to me at all."

"Why do they want to see me?" she asked.

"I think they want to know that you're okay with this. It will happen fast, Winter. We'll probably be married by tomorrow. Mama Irene can do anything on a minute's notice, so I'm sure she can make sure we're married."

"Do you have two bedrooms like I do? I mean, in your cottage is there two bedrooms. One that you sleep in, and one that's empty right now?"

"Yes," he said, cocking his head at her. "I have two bedrooms."

"So, if I stayed in one, you would protect me, but you wouldn't touch me, right? You would stay in your bedroom at night and not come near me unless I say it's okay."

"Right."

"Will I have a ring? I've never had any jewelry," she said quietly. "All the pictures I saw in magazines of ladies getting married, they always had a ring on their left hand. All the women here that are married have rings."

"I'll buy you the biggest ring I can find," he smiled. "Mama Irene has a jeweler that comes out here to let us pick rings out. Saves a lot of time and trouble."

"Okay."

"Okay?" he laughed.

"Okay. Let's go talk to the others."

CHAPTER FOURTEEN

Winter stared at Luke, Cam, and Eric. They were all so tall and big. Taller and bigger than Hiro, but for some reason, today they didn't frighten her. Luke gave her a small smile, and she smiled back at him, still staying a few feet away but closer than she'd ever been.

"He said he'd give me a ring and everything," she said to the men. "That means it's real. It will be a real wedding, a real marriage, right?"

"Yes," said Eric, nodding with a small grin, "but you need to know that in the eyes of the church and in the eyes of the law until you two consummate your relationship, it can be easily broken."

"Consummate?" She repeated the word, scrunching her nose as she spoke. She looked from Eric to Hiro, then back again.

"He means," said Ally, "that you would need to sleep together and have sex. That means that you have truly become man and wife."

"Hiro said he wouldn't make me," she said, staring at the group. "He promised he wouldn't force me. You won't force me, will you? You won't let them watch?" Hiro swallowed, tears filling his eyes. He desperately wanted to help this woman, but her fear was consuming her.

"I won't make you, Winter. Ever. And believe me, no one will ever be watching us if it should happen with your consent. But if someone asks you, you have to lie to them and say that we sleep in the same bed, and we have sex. We'll need to make sure that your bed is made every morning and that you have a few things in my bedroom so that it looks like we're a married couple."

"But we will be a married couple, right?" The perplexed look on her face was almost comical. Hiro was getting nowhere.

"Let me try," said Ace. "You will be married. You will be Mrs. Tanaka. You will have separate rooms, but a few of your things should be in his room in case a lawyer or judge comes to make sure the marriage is legal if Demon says that you are his, not Hiro's. When you introduce yourself to people, you will tell them that you are Mrs. Tanaka. If they ask you if you've consummated the relationship, in other words, had sex or made love, you need to say 'yes.' Can you do that?"

"Okay."

"Okay?" repeated Hiro in frustration.

"Yes. Okay, I'll marry you, and I'll live in the other bedroom and leave some of my things in your room, and I'll tell everyone that we had sex. Should it be lots of sex or just a little?" Hiro rubbed his eyes.

"Whatever you want to tell them is fine," he said calmly.

Mama Irene entered the auditorium, the whispers of a wedding reaching her ears like a bat signal.

"Hi, Mama Irene. I'm Mrs. Tanaka, and I've had a lot of sex with Hiro, and we sleep in the same room." The groans of the men confused her, and she looked around the room, afraid she'd made a mistake.

"Is that so?" she smiled. "Well, you're a lucky girl, and he's a very lucky man. Now, what do you say you come with me, and we'll get you fitted for a wedding dress. The priest will be here at ten tomorrow, Hiro. Wear your uniform. We don't have time for tuxedos. The jeweler will be here at five. Meet us at the big house."

"Yes, Mama Irene," he said, nodding. He watched as she led Winter from the room, then turned to the others. "How did she know?"

"Don't ask," said Gaspar. "We've speculated for years that she has the rooms bugged, but we can't find them."

Noah just grinned at the spirits standing behind him. He knew exactly how she always knew. Because her spies were invisible, dead, and undetectable, except to only a few.

"Hiro? I sure hope you've thought about this, brother. That woman is nowhere near ready for an adult relationship, and she may not be for years. Are you ready for that? I mean, you're a good man, but years without sex and her lying across the hallway from you?"

"I will be fine," he said, smiling at his friend. "I like Winter. I may even love her. I'm not sure. Sacrificing myself for her is a cause I'm willing to embrace. She deserves a life without fear, and if I can provide that for her, then I will."

"You're a special man, brother," said Aiden. "I always knew you were the best of all of us, and I think this just proves it."

"I'm not better than anyone," he said, taking a seat. "My grandfather believed that patience wasn't just a virtue. It was a necessity. Timing is everything in life. You calling me to help out with Stevens was good timing. You offering me the job to come here was good timing. Winter allowing me to come near her, to speak with her was good timing.

"Now, I'm lucky enough to be standing here, willing to marry that beautiful, fragile woman. If I have her in my life, but for just a moment, a precious, perfect moment, it will all be worth it. And if I were to be lucky enough to kill Demon with my bare hands, my life will be complete."

"Like I said," smiled Aiden, "a better man than me."

CHAPTER FIFTEEN

Winter gently touched the lace bodice of the gown. It was the finest, prettiest thing she'd ever seen in her entire life. Thanks to the pond, the scars on her torso were gone, and the neckline revealed a lovely round bosom.

"It's so beautiful," she whispered.

"That's because you're beautiful," smiled Mary. "You're a lovely young woman, and Hiro is a very lucky man."

"No, he's not," she said, shaking her head. "He's very unlucky to like someone like me. Just because he's nice and a hero, the h-e-r-o word, not his name, he's going to marry me and be stuck with someone that can't consummate the marriage." Mary smiled at the young woman.

"One day, you'll feel well enough to do that. One day, you'll wake up and be ready to take another step forward. I mean, look at all the steps you've taken here. You barely spoke to anyone when you arrived. Now, you speak to everyone. You wouldn't look at the men, and now you've just come from an auditorium full of them. You wouldn't let anyone touch you, and now you let Hiro hug you, and others touch your arm or hand.

"One day," said Mary, "you will wake up and walk across the hallway to his bedroom and crawl between the sheets. You may not be naked, but you will be brave enough to reach for him, to hold him. One day, Winter. One day at a time."

"He deserves more than I can give right now, but I want to try. I want so desperately to give him what he needs."

"And why do you think that is, child?" asked Mama Irene.

"I think because I really like him. Maybe even love him, but I'm not sure. I want him to feel the same about me."

"Hiro cares enough for you that he will wait until you're ready to truly be his wife," said Irene. "When you're ready, he'll be ready, trust me." There was a soft knock on the door, and Matthew opened it to see Winter in the lovely gown.

"Well, now, aren't you the prettiest picture I've ever seen," he smiled. "I do believe we got another grandchild gettin' married, Mama."

"We do."

"Who?" said Winter with a confused expression. Matthew and Irene laughed.

"Child, we think of everyone here as ours. You and Hiro, you're like our own children or grandchildren. We love you, Winter. You belong here, with us, and now you'll be part of Hiro's life."

"I've never had parents or grandparents. I don't even know my mother's name."

"If you want someone to walk you down the aisle, just let me know," said Mama Irene. "Usually, a father would do that, but maybe someone here, other than Hiro, has touched your heart in a way that makes them special."

"Yes," she smiled. "I know who to ask."

It was a few hours later that they sat at the dining room table picking out rings. Hiro chose a plain gold band with a matching black rubber band to wear when he was working. Winter thought it was very nice of him to think about that. He said he would keep the real wedding band on a chain around his neck, so that she would always be close to his heart.

"Which one?" he smiled.

"I like them both," she said, looking at the rings. The first was a diamond solitaire with diamonds down the side of the band and a diamond wedding band. The other was a beautiful, soft blue topaz with diamonds around it and down the band as well.

"Which one really speaks to you?" asked the jeweler.

"I think this one."

"The diamonds," he nodded. "Excellent choice. I believe this one is already in your size. You have very tiny hands."

Hiro took the engagement ring and knelt in front of Winter. He placed the ring on her finger and smiled up at her.

"Winter Cole, I'm officially asking you to marry me. Will you say yes?"

"I did say yes," she said in confusion. Hiro laughed, the chuckles of those around them filling the room. "Oh, right. Yes, I'll marry you."

"Can I hug you?" he asked. The jeweler stared at the young couple but just shook his head.

"Yes. Please." He held Winter to his chest, kissing the top of her head. "Will you kiss me like you did before? At the pond?"

Hiro smiled and nodded, lowering his mouth slowly towards her. He gently placed his lips against hers and just held there. She turned her head slightly, moving her lips a little, and then he felt her tongue touch his lips. Opening his mouth somewhat, he let her take control. When she touched her tongue to his, she giggled.

"That feels weird," she laughed.

"It felt wonderful," smiled Hiro. "Thank you."

"Alright, you two, people are waitin' in the cafeteria to celebrate," said Mama Irene. "Winter? They might cheer real loud, honey. Are you gonna be okay with that?"

"I think so," she said, nodding and smiling at the older woman. "Thank you for warning me."

It was exactly as Irene had described. They walked in, and Hiro held up their joined hands, so everyone could see her engagement ring. At first, they only clapped softly. When Winter smiled at them, they clapped louder and cheered.

"You're doing great," said Hiro.

"It's different. I know that now. They're cheering because they like us and care for us, not because they want someone to be hurt."

"That's right, baby."

Winter pulled him toward a table, and he simply followed, wondering what was up her sleeve. Code, Sly, Suzette, Hannah, Ace, and Charlie looked their way.

"Congratulations, you two," said Sly.

"Thank you," said Winter. She turned to look at Ace. "I know that you thought I didn't listen to you that day we were walking, but I did. I'm sorry for what happened to you. I do understand. You know that. What you said made sense to me. The two men who helped you both rode motorcycles. These men, all of you, who have helped me, all ride motorcycles. That doesn't define a bad man."

"That's right, Winter. That's exactly right," said Ace.

"I need someone to walk me down the aisle," she said matter-of-factly. Ace dropped his fork, staring up at her. "It should be you. You're the only one that understands what it was like. You're the only one who knows what it's like to be free of that cage."

"Winter, I'm honored. Are you sure? I mean, what about Matthew or George or one of the other old guys?"

"I heard that, asshole," said Ghost, smiling at the group. "Sounds to me like she's picked the right person."

"Then, yes," said Ace. "I would be honored to walk you down the aisle." The entire cafeteria watched the events unfold, wiping tears from their eyes.

"I read," she said, turning to face them, "that a bride has to have people stand with her. Can I have everyone stand with me?" Mama Irene laughed, nodding her head.

"Well, you can have as many as you want, honey."

"I want them all," she said. "You've all been kind and patient with me. All of you. Keegan and Tinley, I want you as my best maids."

"Matrons of honor," whispered Hiro.

"Right, matrons of honor. I guess that's all," she said quietly. "Did I get it all right?"

"You got it all right, honey," said Hiro, kissing her sweetly in front of everyone. Winter was so unfazed she didn't even blush. She simply kissed him back and smiled. Turning to Ashley, she spoke.

"I think I'm getting better."

"I think you're definitely getting better, honey. Good job."

CHAPTER SIXTEEN

At precisely ten a.m., Winter walked toward Hiro, leaning on the arm of Ace. The slim column dress fit her petite frame beautifully, her perfectly shaped breasts peeking from the neckline. Mama Irene loaned her a strand of pearls with a diamond cluster hanging from it and pearls at her ears. Her dark hair, now cut and shaped by Keegan, still hung down her back in sweeping curls.

Hiro took in a deep breath seeing her, seemingly float, down the aisle toward him. His uniform was laden with heavy medals and ribbons, bringing the eyes of his teammates to his chest. They all had their fair share of hardware, but Hiro had been like a star quarterback on a failing team. He had two purple hearts, multiple commendation medals, rows of ribbons. It was astounding.

"It's your wedding day, so I won't kick your ass," growled Cam, "but we're going to talk about that fucking hardware on your chest."

Hiro said nothing, a soft blush creeping into his cheeks. Winter looked so beautiful he couldn't control the emotions building inside. She was a vision of innocence, angelic, and somewhat clueless. For a moment, he wondered if anyone had fully explained to her what was happening and if she understood. His eyes connected with Mama Irene, and he knew the answer. Looking back at Winter, tears trickled down his cheeks as she stood before him.

"Why are you crying? Have you decided not to marry me? It's okay if you don't want to," she blurted out.

There were soft chuckles behind her, Hiro standing in front of her shaking his head. The woman who once refused to speak to anyone was coming into her own and freely speaking without prompt. He knew in his heart that she had a long way to go, but these baby steps were actually giant footprints.

"No, woman, you're just so damn beautiful I can't help myself."

"Oh," she said, frowning. Looking up at him, she smiled. "Oh. Thank you. You're beautiful, too. Is it okay if I say that?"

"It's okay," smiled Hiro

It was only twenty minutes later when the priest proudly announced that they were husband and wife. The audience applauded, and Hiro looked down at Winter.

"What do we do now?" she said, feeling unsure of herself.

"Now, if you don't mind, we're supposed to share a kiss in front of our friends and family."

"Okay. I don't mind." Hiro could only laugh, shaking his head. He leaned forward, gently kissing her as the cheers got slightly louder. Winter stepped back, her breathing heavy as she felt the familiar panic rise. It was Ace that stepped forward, grabbing her hand.

"It's just friends," he said. "Friends and family. That's all." She nodded at the other man, then turned back to Hiro.

"What happens now?"

"Now, we get to dance, eat, have cake, and celebrate. Later, we'll go back to my cottage. Mama Irene and the others placed your things in the spare room. Okay?"

"Okay."

"Okay," he repeated, smiling to himself.

Winter had never been to a function with so many people who were so well behaved. No one fought, no one hurt anyone, the women were dressed, and the men were kind. People danced on the floors, but there were no poles and no cages. It was the most amazing thing she'd ever seen.

The cake was her favorite, chocolate with chocolate icing, and her favorite meal was served, burgers and French fries. It was like a party just for her. And Hiro.

She found herself watching the other couples dance, the way their husbands held them tightly, but not possessively. Their big hands rested at their lower backs protectively. Some held one hand close to his chest. Others simply hugged them.

"Do you want to dance?" asked Hiro.

"I don't know how," she said, staring at him.

"Come on. I'll show you," he said, holding out his hand. She looked at his hand, then up at him. "Trust me, Winter. I won't hurt you."

"I know. I don't want people to laugh at me."

"No one will laugh at you," he said, kissing her nose. He slowly walked her to the middle of the dance floor, turning her so that she was standing in front of him. With one hand firmly on her back, he clasped her other near his shoulder. He kept about two inches of space between them, slowly rocking back and forth to the music.

"This is nice," she said, looking around the room.

"It is. You look beautiful, Winter. Stunning."

"You do too. Stunning, I mean." Hiro tried to hold in the laugh, but he wasn't very successful. "What are all the things on your chest for?"

"Oh, well, when you're in the military, you receive ribbons or medals for doing certain things."

"Like what?"

"Well, like these two are purple hearts. I was wounded in combat. Some of them are for serving in certain conflicts or regions. Others are distinguished service, marksmanship, lots of things."

"And this one?" she asked. Hiro thought about telling her it was nothing, but he didn't want to start their marriage on a lie.

"That's the Medal of Honor."

The room quieted, and all eyes turned to look at Hiro. The seniors, Gaspar, Nine, Ghost, and Ian stepped closer to the young man. They saw his military records when he came to work for RP, but this one had not been on the record. Cam looked at Luke, who was staring at Hiro.

"What does that mean?" she asked, looking at the faces staring at them.

"The Medal of Honor is awarded for conspicuous gallantry and intrepidity at the risk of life above and beyond the call of duty." He recited the definition verbatim from the military handbook.

"I don't know what that means," said Winter quietly.

"It means," said Luke, walking toward them, "that he risked his own life for others. He put his own life at risk to save those around him. Why didn't you tell us, Hiro?"

"It doesn't mean anything here," he said, shrugging. "You're all Medal of Honor winners in my mind. You've all done it but couldn't be recognized because of your spec ops status. It was hidden, quietly tucked away. I did what all of you would do. My team was pinned down, eight men wounded. I carried them to that helicopter, and we got the hell out. That's all."

"You're amazing, Hiro," said Luke. "Don't ever hide that from us. We're proud of you, and you should be proud of yourself. You've got yourself a winner here, Winter." Hiro watched as each man gave him a quick nod of the head. A sign of respect and admiration. He didn't want it, but somewhere inside of him, he realized he needed it from these men. They were important to him.

By midnight, Winter was yawning, and Hiro lifted her in his arms and carried her to his cottage. There was no loud applause, no fanfare, just them walking away as dozens of pairs of eyes watched them, wondering what their fate would hold. Inside his cottage, he set her down and nervously looked around the room.

"Well, I guess all of your things are in the guest room, so you should find everything there. If you need anything, I'm right across the hall. I'll leave the door open in case you get scared or need anything."

"Okay," she said, nodding. "Hiro? Thank you for marrying me. I know it wasn't easy. You don't love me, and that's okay. Maybe when Demon is dead, you can divorce me and have a life."

"Winter, it was my pleasure to marry you, and believe it or not, I like you enough that I know that one day I will be in love with you if I'm not already. Marrying you was the easiest thing I've ever done. One day, when Demon is gone, we'll talk about what we both want and go from there," he smiled.

He kissed her sweetly, then retired to his room, slowly removing most of his clothing. When he got down to his t-shirt and boxers, he grabbed a pair of pajama pants and stepped inside his bathroom. He washed his face, brushed his teeth, and when he turned off the light, he walked back into his room.

Noticing the light on across the hall, he stepped into the hallway and smiled. Winter was dressed in flannel pajama bottoms and top, lying on the floor with her blanket and pillow. So used to sleeping on nothing, she was thrilled just to have these simple pleasures. She was already sound asleep.

Lying in bed, he looked up at the ceiling, staring at the reflections of light from the wind blowing outside, the moon dancing across the room. He was a married man. A married man alone in his bed, but be damned, he was married.

CHAPTER SEVENTEEN

It seemed that overnight, the weather had done a sudden turn. The once chilly winds and low temperatures were now warm and more spring-like. Hiro stared at Winter as she moved around the top of the boat, artfully placing the Mardi Gras masks along the railings. She was wearing a cute little pair of white shorts with flowers on them, her slender, lean legs leading to her bare feet. The bright pink polish on her toes made him smile. Her tank top was snug on her upper body, the curve of her breasts giving him a vision. The girl who once only wore baggy sweatshirts to cover her scars, now felt able to dress like other women.

Not watching where he was going, his toe hit one of the heavy boxes, and he cursed under his breath, falling to the deck.

"Are you okay?" she asked, turning to look at him. Her hair was high on her head in a tight bun, the soft strands blowing in her face. She knelt beside him, touching his knee.

"Uh, yea, I'm okay." He looked at her face and swallowed, the big doe eyes staring back at him.

"Is something wrong? Have I done something wrong?" she asked.

"God, no Winter. You've done nothing wrong. I-I just, I promised we would always be honest with one another."

"Yes."

"I look at you, Winter, and my heart stops. You're so beautiful and sweet. I'm falling in love with you, and I'm not sure whether to be happy about that or scared. I worry that you won't have the same feelings for me, and one day you're going to break my heart."

"You love me?" she asked, staring at him.

"I do. I know that probably scares you, but I don't want to live a life without you in it. I know that you're not ready to be a real married couple yet, and I'll wait forever for you. I just want to know that you won't run away from me."

Winter stared at him, seeing the fear in his eyes. She'd never met a man that was afraid of her, afraid of what she might do. In that moment, in that one clear and perfect moment, she realized how much power she possessed. She possessed the power to crush this man or to be the wife he deserved. Her sessions with Ashley, Bree, Rachelle, and Calla had helped, as well as the session with the other women in her support group. She knew that loving a man could be beautiful and wonderful. She'd read the books they gave her, even watched a few movies they'd suggested.

Hiro was seated on the deck, his arms resting on bent knees. His head was slightly down when Winter opened his clasped hands and kneeled in front of him. She gently pushed his legs to the deck, then sat with her legs on top of his, curling them around his body.

"Winter," he whispered.

"Let me do this," she said. "Let me control this." Hiro nodded, not wanting to spoil the most perfect moment of his life. She scooted closer, her groin pressed against his hard cock. Her eyes went wide, but she didn't panic. Instead, she looked down and stared.

"Am I hurting you?" she asked.

"No," his cracking voice said. "It's not painful in that way. I want release, I need release, but I can do it myself later."

"Is that what you want to do?" she asked innocently.

"No, honey, that's not what I want. I want to make love to my wife, but I will not be an animal and force you."

"Can I make love to you? Can I control everything and decide what happens?" she asked sweetly.

"Yes. If you want, you can always control everything." Winter stood and went below deck, closing the shades of the lower deck. She locked the door and turned to see Hiro at the bottom of the steps, staring at her.

"Will you undress for me?" she asked. He nodded, stripping off his shirt first, then his shorts and boxers. "You're very muscular. It's pretty."

"Baby," he said, shaking his head with a smile. "There is nothing more beautiful than you."

"Your cock is big," she said matter-of-factly. Hiro chuckled, nodding. Winter pulled the tank top over her head, then unhooked her bra and let it fall. She wiggled out of her shorts, and Hiro was surprised to see that she'd taken his suggestion and waxed completely.

"Am I okay? Do you like me still?" she asked.

"I love you more, Winter. You're being so fucking brave." She pointed to the sofa bench, and he laid down, watching her move slowly toward him. Her fingers raked across his legs and upward to his chest. He watched her swallow and then straddle his thighs.

"I get to do this, right?"

"Right," he said with a croak.

Lifting herself, she gripped his cock and slid it into her opening. She felt the heat and wetness coming from her and realized that it was something new, she'd never been wet before. Hiro wasn't sure what he expected, but he didn't expect her to be so tight. She moaned as she lowered herself, her perfect breasts heaving up and down. His hands were clasped behind his head as he tried to prevent himself from reaching for her.

"It feels different with you," she gasped. "It's nicer. My stomach isn't sick. It's fluttering, and I feel like I need to move." Hiro frowned at her and then realized she'd probably never had an orgasm.

"Honey, this will make you feel really good if you move. My penis will rub certain parts of your body and make you obtain an orgasm. The pleasure women get with sex. You just have to move your body in the way that pleases you."

She tried several times to find a rhythm, but each time became frustrated by her awkward movements. It didn't matter to Hiro. He was fucking loving it, but he wanted her to get enjoyment first.

"Can I touch you, Winter? Can I help you move so that you find this enjoyable?" She nodded, and he slowly gripped her hips, rocking her forward and then back.

"Oh," she gasped, "that's wonderful." Hiro chuckled.

"Yea, baby, it is. You're so beautiful, Winter. So damn perfect, and I'm very happy that you're my wife." She instinctively touched her breasts, and her eyes went wide at the sensation.

"Can I touch myself?" she asked.

"Yea, honey. Touching yourself might help you feel the joy. Especially your nipples and down there," he said with a nod of his head. He was so fucking hard right now he was dying, but he wanted her to cum first, feeling their love first.

"Show me," she said breathlessly, "show me everything."

"Are you sure?" he asked. Winter nodded as Hiro sat up, wrapping her legs around him. He continued to guide her hips and felt her body squeeze around him, her back intuitively arching as her body began to shudder with pleasure and release. Hiro jerked his own hips forward, filling her with his seed, then leaned forward, gently taking her lips.

It shouldn't have shocked him, but it did. Winter gripped his hair, taking his mouth, dancing with his tongue as she continued her rocking motion against him.

"Winter, baby," he said, gasping for air, "if you keep doing that, I'm going to get hard all over and will need to do that again."

"Can't we do it more than once? That was wonderful, and I want to feel that again. I've never in my entire life felt that. Can we do it again?" she asked.

"Yea," he laughed, "I'll do it all day if you want."

"I might be sore after all day, but I like the way you do this. It feels amazing, and it's not scary or painful. My whole body was shaking with this energy I've never felt before. You fit me differently. Is that normal?" Hiro tried to control the dark cloud passing through his mind.

"Yea, baby. Every man is different. You and I were meant for one another, Winter. You're so fucking brave, honey. Letting me take control was the bravest thing you've ever done. We're truly married now. You won't have to lie if someone asks if we've had sex."

"Was it sex or lovemaking?" she asked sweetly.

"For me, it was lovemaking, Winter." She stared at him, kissing him once more. Leaning forward, she pressed her breasts against his chest and felt him grow inside her.

"I think it was lovemaking for me, too. Will you keep me now?" she asked. Hiro held her firmly against his chest.

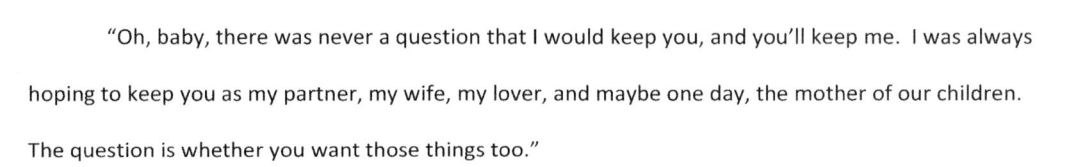

"Oh, baby, there was never a question that I would keep you, and you'll keep me. I was always hoping to keep you as my partner, my wife, my lover, and maybe one day, the mother of our children. The question is whether you want those things too."

"I can have you as all those things?" she asked.

"That's the plan, beautiful. All those things wrapped in one package."

"Okay."

"Okay?" he laughed. "Can I have a little more?"

"Okay, I want to keep you as my husband, my lover, my partner, and maybe one day, the father of our children. Is that okay?" He grinned at her, kissing her once more as he lay her carefully on the bench and began moving inside her.

"Okay."

CHAPTER EIGHTEEN

Hiro and Winter stayed below deck, wrapped around one another, all afternoon. She fell asleep in his arms and would wake wanting to explore his body. When he asked if he could taste her, she was reluctant at first, but staring at his lips, wondered what it would feel like. She wasn't disappointed. However, she did emphasize that she could not do that same for him. Those memories were horrible for her, and she just couldn't do it.

Hiro knew that it would be a stretch for her. He didn't need it. He had her, and she was already changing before his eyes. Walking into the cafeteria, several people turned and smiled, knowing that they'd been on the boat all day with the blinds shut. Winter looked at the room and back at Hiro.

"It's okay," she called out. "We made love a lot, and we're married now." The room broke out in chuckles, and then a light applause that only made her smile.

"I love you," he said, kissing her.

"I know," she smiled. "I love you, too. It's so strange. You're the first person I've ever loved. Will you be the last?"

"I hope I'm the last husband you will ever love, but you'll find that you have enough love to love a friend, like Keegan or Ashley. You'll love Mama Irene and George for the way they help you and the others."

"So, there are lots of kinds of love?" she asked.

"Yea, baby. There are so many kinds of love. It's amazing."

"Are there lots of kinds of hate?"

"No. Sometimes we use hate instead of dislike, but there's only one type of hate. You might dislike broccoli, but you don't hate it. It has no emotion. It's a food. You might be frightened of dogs, but you don't hate them."

"I noticed there are a lot of big dogs here," she said, staring at Sniff and Lucy's table. Five massive dogs were at their feet.

"They're here to protect us," said Hiro. "The dogs know when someone is here that shouldn't be here. If you'll let me, I'll show you how gentle they are."

"Well," she said, standing, "I've been pretty brave today, maybe I can be brave for a while longer." Hiro laughed as they walked toward the K-9s.

"Hey, Sniff, Lucy, my brave new wife would like to meet the dogs and try to become more comfortable with them."

"They're really just big babies," smiled Lucy. "Rogue might be the best to start with." Lucy stood and called Rogue out from beneath the table. The nearly one-hundred-and-seventy-five-pound dog stood, his head above her waist.

"He's really big," whispered Winter feeling a bit of panic rise in her. The club, at one time, had dogs that they would make fight. When they weren't fighting each other, they were fighting for food, and Winter often lost her meal to them.

"He is, but he's a gentle giant unless you're trying to hurt anyone here on the property. Hold your hand out, palm down." Winter did as she was told and waited. "Rogue? Friend." Rogue walked toward the woman and sniffed her hand. He sat back on his hind legs, his nose nudging her palm.

"He wants you to pet him," smiled Hiro. Winter looked at the dog and swallowed, then touched the top of his head.

"He's so soft," she said. "He won't bite me, will he?"

"Never, Winter. Rogue will only go after someone who is trying to hurt you or anyone here on the property." Winter kneeled before the dog, then sat on the cafeteria floor. Rogue immediately took that as a good sign, lying down beside her and placing his head in her lap. Winter laughed, rubbing his soft fur once again.

"His nose is cold," she said.

"Yes, that means he's healthy," said Lucy. She felt the other dogs move from beneath the table, each one moving closer to Winter. One by one, they laid beside her, their heads touching a part of her body. Laughing, she looked up at Hiro.

"I think I want a dog," she said.

"Why don't we see how you do with dog-sitting these monsters first?" he chuckled. He reached for Winter's hand and heard a low growl from Rogue. "Whoa, boy, she's my wife, not yours. I won't hurt her Rogue."

"He's protecting me? Already?" she asked Lucy.

"He latches on quickly, especially to women. He can sense your fear and isn't sure if it's him you're afraid of or Hiro. Rogue is a bit of an alpha male, so he assumes it's Hiro you fear."

Winter stood, the dogs all standing with her. Rogue nudged her hand, flopping it on top of his head. Proudly, he stared at the others, glaring at Hiro.

"Okay, look dog, we have to come to an understanding. I want you to protect her and keep her safe, but she doesn't belong to you," smiled Hiro.

"Are you sure about that?" grinned Sniff. "Why don't you take him with you for a few days, Winter? He'll come back to the center when he's ready, but you can get a sense of what it's like to have a dog around. I promise, he won't ever hurt you."

"I like him. Come boy, let's get some dinner." Winter and Rogue walked toward the food line, his head obediently at her hips.

"Did I just lose my new wife to a dog?" grinned Hiro.

"I don't think so, but you might lose a chunk of your ass in a minute," smiled Sniff, nodding toward the seniors, Eric, Cam, and Luke walking toward them.

"Oh, shit," he muttered.

"Hiro. I trust that you and your bride are off to a good start," said Cam. "Why didn't you tell us, Hiro? Why would you hide that from your service record?"

"It doesn't matter. You hired me based on the other things. I didn't deserve that medal. I did what anyone else would have done."

"No, you didn't," said Ghost. "Son, one of your purple hearts was from that mission. You had a bullet in your leg, Hiro. Those other men, some of them, were hurt less than you, but it was you that went back and carried them to that bird."

"It was my last team, and they didn't know me very well. I'd become known for my use of martial arts and not weapons. I didn't want to start my relationship with them like that, but I didn't have a choice. I couldn't carry a man and fire weapons. I fought off the tangoes, would pick up a man and tell him to cover me, he or my teammate would provide cover, and I'd dump him on the bird. He'd provide cover while I went back, and so on."

"Hiro, we're not mad, brother. It's fucking amazing what you did," said Luke. "We operate on full disclosure and trust here. Just don't withhold anything in the future, okay?"

"Yea, I'm sorry. Of course."

"You're badass, Hiro," smiled Nine. "Fucking wish you'd been on my team a lifetime ago, but I'm damn happy you're here now."

"Me too," he grinned, looking back at Winter feeding Rogue pieces of steak. "I think she's going to be okay."

"I'm so fucking happy for you, Hiro," said Eric. "I was worried when you agreed to marry her. It could have gone either way, brother. Another proven incident of what kind of man you are."

"No, it was an easy decision to make. She's amazing and beautiful and innocent and wise all at the same time. There's a wisdom to Winter that none of us has or can understand. She's completely unaware of her effect on those around her. She has no emotional intelligence in most situations because she hasn't been taught even the simplest of things. But I think she knows more than she thinks she does. In fact, I think she knows more than she thinks she does about Los Muertos."

"What do you mean?" asked Gaspar.

"I mean, a club like Los Muertos wouldn't be searching for one woman for more than five years. Women are a dime a dozen to them. There's something that she knows or that she has, that they want. I just don't know what it is."

"You might be right," frowned Cam. "All the more reason to make sure that woman doesn't leave this property."

"No shit," muttered Hiro. He turned to look at the men and grinned. "Are we good?"

"We're good, brother," smiled Luke. "Fucking Medal of Honor." Hiro shrugged.

"It looks good on the uniform."

CHAPTER NINETEEN

Michael Bodwick sat across from Director Tony Whitlow of the FBI and Director Art Comstock of Homeland. He'd listened to their two-hour bullshit session on why RP shouldn't touch Demon and the Los Muertos and then decided he'd had enough. He could smell political, ass-saving bullshit a mile away. Seated beside him were Doug and Miguel, almost as frustrated as he was.

"Directors, let me just stop you there," said Bodwick, raising his hand. "I've heard a lot of bullshit in my day, but your lengthy monologue was award-winning, oxygen-sucking shit."

"Mr. Bodwick!"

"Don't Mr. Bodwick me, asshole. If you like, we can get the president on the line as well as the heads of the military branches. You're not telling me something, and I want to know what it is."

Silence greeted him as the men stared down at their files. Doug didn't have a good feeling about this at all. He looked at Miguel, who smiled his crooked smile and winked at him.

"Perhaps I'll start," said Miguel. There was barely a trace of the slur once predominant in his speech after the stroke. The only evidence was a slight downturn of the right side of his mouth. "I'm sure you gentlemen are aware of my colorful past. I've spent the better part of thirty years attempting to erase it and do right by my family, the RP family.

"I left that life, but I didn't sever all connections. In fact, it's often good to have enemies in your back pocket, just in case. Some of my enemies have become my friends in a manner of speaking. I called these friends, and they had quite a tale to tell." Miguel waited to see if the Directors would offer up anything, but when they didn't, he simply smiled and continued.

"Miroslav Vicenko is the premier buyer of drugs and women in Eastern Europe. He provides women for businessmen and murderers alike. In fact, his stable is usually labeled by age, color, size, and use. The less used, the more money.

"His drugs are some of the most advanced in the world. It seems Vicenko fancies himself a bit of a chemist in a weird sort of way. Now, I don't know the man personally, but I know his brother. Mikael Vicenko parted ways with his brother twenty years ago. I'm not saying all of his business dealings are legitimate, but he doesn't deal in flesh or drugs.

"Miroslav gets the bright idea that he could run women through an indoctrination boot camp of sorts, using the Los Muertos. It seems he saw them in action at a bike rally where he was supplying women to the guests. Demon practically tore apart one of his women, and in an odd way, Miroslav was impressed. Los Muertos was to train the women to take physical and sexual punishment in extreme, only to be sent to him to be abused far worse by his disgusting clients."

"Mr. Santos, you're not telling us anything we don't already know," said Director Comstock. His face was pale, a bead of perspiration gathering at his temple. Santos had him right where he wanted him.

"Really? And yet, you didn't stop him. I wonder why," smiled Santos.

"Careful, Mr. Santos," he snarled.

"Why? Do you plan to bring up something from thirty years ago while I resided in another country? I'm an old man, Director. You don't scare me. Let me tell you why you haven't moved on Los Muertos yet.

"You both have daughters. I believe Director Comstock, yours is just fifteen, and yours, Director Whitlow, is sixteen. They have been held in a small town outside of Gomel, Belarus, for almost a year now. They must be terrified."

"Mr. Santos…"

"Los Muertos has told Miroslav that they are not to be touched or you will come down on the club, which of course would mean that you will come down on him. Until then, they are kept safe and warm, given food and clothing, but one wrong move on your parts and your daughters will enter a world from which they will never emerge."

"Shut the fuck up!" yelled Whitlow.

"What I don't understand is why you haven't dispatched a team to get those girls out. You have the resources to send a SEAL team, Rangers, CIA. Hell, you could have called RP, and we would have done it for you. Yet, you didn't." Miguel let the seconds tick by on the big round clock on the wall. The ticking was infuriating and lulling all at the same time.

"Shall I continue?" Their faces were red, sweat beading on their foreheads. "Never mind, that was rhetorical. You didn't go in or send someone in because if you didn't want the videotape of the two of you fucking a thirteen-year-old girl to be sent to the media. A child. Younger than your child."

"Oh, God," muttered Whitlow. "Please, you don't understand."

"Then help us understand," said Bodwick.

"He's right. Originally, we thought Los Muertos could help us get to Miroslav. We went to this meeting with Demon and the others. Things were getting out of control, the bodies of the women they'd gone too far with, the ones they'd killed were piling up, and people were taking notice. We needed to make them understand this couldn't continue. They were only supposed to be feeding us information on Miroslav, and we would leave them alone on the drug running. We never agreed to give them free reign to murder children.

"They offered us food and drink, and we took it. It was stupid. A dumb fucking rookie move, but we took it. Neither of us knew what we were doing. It was as if we were floating above ourselves. I woke up, and this little girl was lying between us. She was naked and bleeding everywhere."

"She was crying for her mother," said Comstock. "By the time we were lucid enough to stand, we realized that they'd been filming us. All of it. About once a month, photos or a video clip show up in our mailbox. When we threatened to turn them in anyway, they took our girls."

"And you were too fucking cowardly to step forward and admit your damn mistake? Instead, you put your daughters at risk and let those animals continue to abuse women and children. Do I have that right?" asked Bodwick.

"Yes," said Comstock quietly, "you have that right."

"Well, listen to me, you cowardly piece of shit, we're going to go in and save your daughters. We're going to bring them home, and then we're going to destroy Los Muertos. I can't help you save your damn jobs, but I don't really give a fuck about that. Ironically, I care about your kids because I have a daughter. I know what that fear is like. So, we'll do this for you, but so help me God, if you get in our way, if you don't cooperate, I will kill you myself."

"I realize who you work with now, Bodwick, but you have no idea what these men are capable of. They have no rules, no morals, no qualms about killing, raping, anything to get what they want," said Comstock.

"And yet you still did business with them," he sneered. "That says far more about you than about them. Stay out of our way, and we'll have your daughters home in no time. If you're helpful, we might even see if we can wipe out the videos." The two men looked at one another. A glimpse, brief though it might be, flickered across their faces.

"What else can you tell us about them?" asked Bodwick. He hoped that they would give him something about Winter.

"You know what we know. They have no loyalty whatsoever. If anyone crosses them, they kill them, period. Demon killed his own wife."

"His wife? We didn't find that he was ever married," said Doug.

"We heard all this second-hand, in bits and pieces, but it wasn't recorded as a marriage. It was common law. He took the girl from a high school football game when she was just fifteen. He really likes blondes, and she was a cute little blonde."

"Yea, we know," murmured Miguel.

"He ravaged that poor kid. Kept her tied to his bed for years. Let some of the other guys use her as well. She got away, ran back home for help, pregnant. Her folks refused to help her. She had no other option but to go back."

"She was pregnant?" asked Bodwick, swallowing. "When? When was this?"

"About twenty-five years ago or so. He killed her after she gave birth to the kid, abused her so horribly, she died from hemorrhaging so badly. That's the story we heard anyway."

"Boy or girl?" asked Doug.

"A girl. She got away from what we know. He asked for our help in finding her, but we said we didn't have the manpower. Besides, he was abusing the kid as well. Raping her, beating her, giving her to his men. We learned the story from one of the older bikers while he was wasted. Said that Demon was obsessed with his own kid and would do anything to get her back."

"He's her father," whispered Miguel, tears springing to his eyes. "He's her fucking father."

"You know her?" asked Comstock.

"You let her stay there knowing what he was doing to her?" asked Bodwick.

"We couldn't do a damn thing, and you know it. We started doing business with him about seven years ago. The kid was a teenager and too far gone to save. He was fucking brutal with her, but you couldn't get near her. He kept her in a cage above the floor. When I asked him why he treated his own flesh and blood that way, he just laughed and said it was because he loved her."

"I'm going to save your kids," said Bodwick, "and then I'm going to give my team your names and addresses. You fucking animals had the ability to save that kid or at least try. How many others were there? Huh? How many!"

Neither man answered, simply staring at their folded hands on the table.

"Let's go," said Doug. "We've got two frightened little girls waiting for a rescue."

CHAPTER TWENTY

"I can't tell her that," said Hiro, shaking his head, tears rolling down his face. "I can't tell her that evil son-of-a-bitch is her father. That he killed her own mother. She'll crumble."

"She has to find out sooner or later, Hiro. It doesn't have to be now, but talk to Rachelle and Ashley, see what they say," said Luke.

"Fucking Belarus," said Eric. "That place is a fucking powder keg, especially where Gomel is sitting. It's prime for rebels coming from Russia, Yugoslavia, Ukraine. It's a fucking mess."

"It is," said Cam, "but we're fucking getting those kids out. Ace? You have visuals yet?"

"Yes," he said, tapping a few keys. The screen lit up with an aerial view of a rural farm. "I'm not sure if Comstock and Whitlow were idiots or just scared to death to do anything, but it was easy to locate. The weekly phone calls and video chats were easily traced back to the farm. There are six men that guard the property. They come and go for food and other things, but no one else has come onto the property.

"About two hours ago, two young girls were brought out of the cellar door, here," he said, pointing to the screen. "They were both dressed in sweatsuits and had tennis shoes on, but that's it. No coats, nothing, and it's fucking cold there right now. They were given five minutes to just get fresh air, then shoved back into the cellar. I don't know if there are additional men down there, but the girls appear unharmed."

"What about the roads, Ace?" asked Cam.

"Just one road in and out, but if you look to the side of the house, there are three dirt bikes. Either this is their mode of transportation, or there are trails that they know of for a quick escape."

"Where are Miroslav's men?" asked Eric.

"There's another property I found about ten miles from this one. It's larger, and there's a reason for that." He panned out on the computer, moving the screen to the next house. It looked like a mansion, albeit rundown. "You can see the luxury cars parked out front, at least a dozen. This is where Miroslav is sitting. Just since you sent the message from D.C., three vans filled with girls have pulled into that house. I don't think that's where he keeps them, but that's where he brings them."

They watched the house, men with AKs wrapped around their arms walking the perimeter. The front door opened, and a robust, bald man walked out with a girl over his shoulder. She was naked, whip marks on her buttocks and back.

"Is that live?" asked Hiro.

"It is," growled Ace.

"We can't let that house stand," said Dalton, staring at his friends.

Nine, Ghost, Gaspar, Ian, Trak, Eric, Alec, and the rest of the seniors sat in the back row as usual. They looked at one another and grinned.

"Hey, uh, just a suggestion," said Baptiste, "but what do you say to letting the seniors take on the big house while you boys rescue the girls."

"Dad," said Cam, staring at Nine, "you promised Mom you wouldn't do these big international jobs any longer."

"I know. I know, but it's about kids, and she'll understand," he said, frowning. "I tell you what, a few of us will stay back, but let some of us old guys have fun."

"Besides," said Antoine, "this isn't the first time we've faced Miroslav. We owe him one, and payback, as we all know, is a bitch."

Cam, Luke, and Eric stared from their fathers back to one another. Looking at Hiro, he nodded toward him.

"Hiro? This is about your wife. You should make the decisions here," said Cam.

"What? Fuck no! I'm not making that choice. What if something happens to them?"

"Thanks for the vote of confidence, Junior," smirked Tailor.

"That's not what I meant. Look, I know we need to get all of those girls out of there, especially the two at the farm before they're forced into the general population of girls. But risking your lives for that, I'm not so sure. Just drop me near the farm, and I'll get the girls out."

"What the fuck are you talking about?" said Luke. "Did you not hear us last time? We are a team, Hiro. A fucking team. We do this together. We know that you're some sort of secret ninja master, and you're damn capable, but you don't do this alone."

"You're right," he said, nodding, "I'm sorry. I just don't want anyone hurt because of me."

"It's not because of you, Hiro," said Miller. "These men chose a path that was only going to end one way. They never anticipated that we would cross their paths and fuck everything up. Now, I'm tired of sitting on my ass and only doing fluff duties. I might be old, but I'm not fucking dead. I'm still an operator, and so are my brothers, all of them."

"Full of yourself much, Uncle Pierre," smiled Luke.

"Yea, boy, I am," he grinned. Luke held up his hands, laughing.

"Alright, we'll split into teams. A few will stay with the birds and comms, guiding us by the drones. A small team will rescue the girls at the farmhouse, and the rest will go to the big house. Nine, Gaspar, Ian, Ghost, Wilson, Gabriel, Bull, and Doc will stay here. Once we have the two girls on the bird, we'll move to help you guys at the big house. We have no idea how many men are there."

"Oh, man," said Tailor, clapping, "this is gonna be so much fun!"

Hiro shook his head, smiling up at the men who were his new family. He looked back at the folder containing the information about Demon and Winter and frowned.

"How am I going to tell her?" he asked.

"Tell me what?" said Winter, standing in the door. She held a tray of King Cakes that Mama Irene had instructed her to bring to the men for their break. She set the big tray down, the pastries filling the room with the warm aroma of cinnamon and sugar.

"Winter," he said quietly.

"What do you need to tell me?" Hiro swallowed, looking out at the men.

"Nothing, just that I'll be gone a few days on a mission. I need for you to stay here and not leave the property, okay?"

"Okay," she smiled. "Enjoy the cakes." She kissed his cheek, leaving the room with a bounce in her step. When he turned, the stares of a hundred men made him shrivel.

"Fuck. I just told my first lie to my wife."

CHAPTER TWENTY-ONE

"Don't beat yourself up over this, Hiro," said Ashley. "Sometimes keeping things from your spouse is the right thing to do, especially if it's going to do more harm than good. You're doing this for all the right reasons. One day, when she's more secure and confident in who she is, you can share it. I think it's okay that you didn't do it now."

"Really?" he asked, emotions bubbling to the surface.

"Really," smiled Rachelle. "I couldn't agree more with Ashley. At this point, what would it do? What purpose would it serve? She'd be more confused and devastated knowing that piece of information. Plus, she's just finding out who she is, what she can become, and if she knows that Demon is her father, what will that do to her? I can't even fathom that."

"That's what I'm worried about," he said, frowning. "What if she finds out? What if somehow, someone on this property says something to her?"

"No one will say anything," said Rachelle. "The guys know to not share this with their wives. God, I look at my father and Mac, and I just can't even begin to imagine them doing anything so horrible. It's a special kind of broken that would do this, Hiro. I know that you're aware he's a dangerous man, but he's psychologically unstable. He sees Winter as property that belongs to him. I don't think it even registers that she's blood."

"Okay," he said, nodding. "I'm sorry to have rushed in here and bombarded you both with my concerns. I was just so worried I would do or say the wrong thing."

"Hiro, take a seat," said Rachelle, waving to the empty chair. He nodded, taking the seat across from the two women.

"Hiro, you've been solely responsible for bringing Winter to life. She's been here almost four months now. The first month, she refused to even leave the salon or the efficiency above it. When she was scared that someone would break in or see her, she agreed to a cottage on the property.

"Since then, in that span, you've been able to get her to communicate with you, look at you, touch you, and even marry you. She trusts you like no one else in her life. I want you to think about what a gift that is considering how men have treated her."

"You're special, Hiro," said Ashley. "You have a talent that is beyond your abilities as a soldier, or warrior, as savior. You said once that your grandfather instilled in you the need for patience."

"Yes," he nodded. "He would make me wait forever for things, donuts, walks, anything so that I would learn to enjoy the moment. That's what I've tried to do with Winter. Enjoy the little moments, the little wins."

"That's exactly what you've done, honey," said Ashley, reaching for his hand. "You've shown more patience than any man or woman I've ever known. That patience is laden with love and respect which makes it all the more precious. Use that gift of yours to bring her peace, not strife, Hiro."

He nodded, thinking about what she'd said. Grandfather always said that patience was the center of silence. He'd learned to be quiet by showing patience. He didn't rush to the enemy. He waited patiently, silently, until the time was right. That's how he could sneak up on people, frighten them so easily, and he suspected it's exactly what Trak, Joseph, and Nathan did as well.

Since the moment he'd laid eyes on Winter, he knew that she would be the woman that captured his heart. He was patient, waiting for her to see him and know that he was there, that he wouldn't harm her. That patience paid off the day she gave him her hand in marriage.

"Thank you, both of you. I won't let her know. Not right now. Maybe one day, but today it won't change anything except to complicate her world more." He looked out the windows of the clinic, the sun shining down. The buds of spring were already coming to the surface. Life was beginning anew. "Will you check in on her while we're gone? I know it will only be a day or two, but still."

"Of course, we will, honey. We'll all be sticking close together. You boys go do you, and we'll be just fine."

Hiro jogged back toward the main property, using this opportunity to get an additional run into his day. He spotted Winter sitting on her favorite bench and waved to her, running in her direction.

"Hi, baby," he said, leaning down and kissing her.

"I like when you do that," she smiled. "The way you call me sweet names like baby or honey or sweetie. I really like it when you call me your love or your wife. One of the books I read said that when a man really loves his wife, he isn't afraid to show her every day."

"I'll never be afraid to tell you what you mean to me, Winter. You're all those things and more," he said, pulling her to stand. He wrapped his arms around her, kissing her again.

"I think you see things in me that others don't or won't, but it's why I love you, Hiro. I've had a lot of conversations with Rachelle, Bree, Ashley, and Calla, as well as Mama Irene, Mary, Erin, Lauren, and the others. I said once that I wasn't sure what love feels like, what it looked like, but you've taught me that. You've shown me what it is and opened my eyes to what it is not. What I feel for you is love. I know that more every day, and I hope one day that we'll be able to give that love to a child."

"Oh, sweetie, my love," he grinned, "I hope for that too, but there's no rush. We'll get used to one another, do things as a couple first, then add in a child if it's right. How does that sound?"

"Perfect," she said, kissing him. She lay her head against his chest and rocked back and forth. "I'm going to miss you when you're gone. I love how you make love to me, how you always make me feel safe. I love waking up to you."

"Me, too, honey. We're leaving later this evening. Why don't you and I go take a hot bath together and make love before I leave? You control it all."

"I think I like it when you take a little control," she smiled. "I've learned that it's not awful."

"Not awful? Wound my heart," he laughed. "I know what you mean. Let's go, beautiful. I want to make my wife happy before I leave."

"You'll come back for me, right, Hiro?"

"Always, Winter. Always."

CHAPTER TWENTY-TWO

Frank smiled at the five men standing at the front of the auditorium. He'd put out the call, and Fitch and Bron answered immediately, driving all night and bringing three of their friends with them, all Marines. The men stood at parade rest, their hands behind their backs, and Frank just shook his head.

"Fuck yea," laughed Rory, "Semper fi, brothers."

"Semper fi," they grinned. One of the men leaned toward Fitch, whispering.

"Who is that?" he asked.

"That, my brother, is *the* Master Sergeant Rory Baine, USMC, retired," grinned Fitch.

"Oh, fuck," said one of the younger men. "Sir, it's an honor to meet you, sir."

"What's your name, son?" asked Rory.

"Uh, my name is Jordan Rory Callahan," he grinned. "My father served with you, sir. Sergeant Michael Callahan."

"I remember big Mike," grinned Rory looking at the son. Fuck, he was old enough to know a Marine with a son as old as his nieces and nephews. "You're built like your old man, bigger."

"Yes, sir, thank you, sir," said Jordan, straightening. "My middle name was in honor of you, sir."

"First, stop calling me fucking 'sir,' my name is Rory. That's it. Second, that's a huge fucking honor. I wish your old man had told me."

"He died, sir. I mean, Rory. He died only a few months after I was born."

"Fuck, I'm sorry, Jordan. Really, I am. I had no idea."

"It's okay. My mom remarried a really good man, and she was happy. I followed in Dad's footsteps, and I've been happy as well. I'm hoping one day to come here." Rory could only nod. He'd watch the young man and see how he does for a few days.

The door to the auditorium opened, and Mama Irene walked in with George, Matthew, and Mary, all four of them wheeling carts filled with sandwiches, chips, cookies, and drinks.

"I heard we got guests, and you're gonna need food to plan a mission," she smiled. The five new men stared at the tiny woman and knew immediately who she was. "Now, let me look at you, boys. My name is Irene, but everyone calls me Mama, Mama Irene, or just Irene. No ma'am. No Mrs. Understand?"

"Yes, ma'am," came the chorus as the others all groaned.

"Now, what did I just say?" she fussed with her hands on her hips. She shook her head and looked at Frank. "Frank? Introduce your little friends."

"Grandma, they're... never mind. Grandma, this is Patrick Fitch and Bron Jones, the two men who helped me with Lane."

"Oh, now for that, you boys get slices of my famous lemon cake."

"Hey, that's not fair," said Tailor, frowning at Mama Irene.

"You get more than your share of everything around here, Tailor Bongard. Don't make me start rationing you."

"Yes, ma'am." Irene turned to yell at him, but Tailor's big smile just made her laugh.

"Dude, that's fucking Tailor Bongard," whispered Callahan.

"Yea," laughed Fitch, "we know. Mama Irene, these men are three fellow Marines who gave up their leave to come out and help. We all hope to be part of your family one day. This is Jordan Callahan, Ryker Dumas, and Justice Zachary."

"Well, now," said Irene, stepping back. "You're fine-lookin' young men. Tall, strong, handsome. Yes, sir, you'll do just fine. And, Fitch, don't insult me again. You step foot on this property, you're family."

"Yes, Mama Irene," smiled Fitch.

"Okay, you boys, eat." The four elderly people left the room, the five new Marines staring at one another.

"What the hell did she mean by that? You'll do just fine."

"You don't wanna know," laughed Frank. Lane opened the doors and immediately ran toward Fitch and Bron, hugging them fiercely. The two men looked down at her, then at the room of men, confusion filling their faces.

"I guess they did good with my surgery if you two don't recognize me," she smiled.

"Holy shit," whispered Bron. "It's Stephanie. I mean, Lane. Holy shit."

"Damn girl, you look awesome," said Fitch, hugging her again. "You could do a helluva lot better than that big asshole over there."

"Sorry, boys, I'm married to that big asshole now. Besides, I kinda love him."

"No accounting for taste," smiled Bron. "You look amazing, Lane. I'm so damn glad to see you happy and healthy."

"I owe a lot of that to you," she smiled. She turned to the other three men and nodded. "No time for introductions. I know you're busy, but I'm Lane Robicheaux, married to Frank. I'll see you guys later." She kissed her husband, then hugged her father and uncle.

"Wait," said Callahan, "are they related to her?"

"Titus Quinn is her father, and Rory is her uncle."

"You're a dumbass," smirked Justice, shaking his head at Frank. Only someone insane would marry the daughter of Titus Quinn and niece to Rory Baine.

"Can we get down to business, gentlemen?" said Luke, filling his plate and taking a seat. "We're going to leave a handful of our own men back, including a few of the Robicheaux cousins. Most of them served at least one tour in the military, but their real value comes in that they know this land better than anyone other than those that live here. They're familiar with the swamps, the hidden places we've created, and trust me when I tell you this, they're all fucking great shots."

"Your primary responsibilities," said Eric, standing in front of the group and pointing to a spot on the property map, "will be to keep the women and children safe here, at the Sugar Lodge." Ryker looked up and up and up, staring at the huge man in front of him.

"He's gotta be related to big boy in the back, right?" he whispered to Jordan.

"Sound carries in this room," frowned Eric. "And yes, I'm big boy's son, Eric Bongard. You boys have size as well, but we seem to attract men who are bigger than the one before. Maybe one day, if you join our little family, you can be on our very special team. Let me introduce you to Team Big. Gentlemen, stand when I call your name." The Marines turned to watch as Eric called each of the names.

"Noah and Noa," he grinned as the men stood. "Dad, Alec, Max, Titus, Parker, Zulu, and Skull. Technically, Frank, myself, and Rory qualify, but it's an exclusive club." Eric grinned as the men in front of him swallowed. They understood that these men were special due to their training, but given their size, anything was possible.

"Holy shit," muttered Justice. "Uh, when can I apply to work here."

"Show us what you have, and we'll talk," said Luke. "There is nothing more important than our families, nothing. Our wives, kids, the people who work on this property are all family to us. The Sugar Lodge is a converted sugar mill hidden at the back of the property. It has a fully working kitchen, dormitory-style bunks, televisions, and a weapons room that would rival the White House. The four people you just met, my grandmother, grandfather, George, and Mary, are all highly capable of shooting a man. Believe me, my grandmother has."

"Cool," smiled Fitch. "Hey, we thought we'd give you guys a leg up on our drive over. Thanks to your man, Code, we found the clubhouse in Arizona. We thought we'd do a little recon, but there was nothing to see. It was empty, no people inside at all, but they'd been there recently. The electricity was off, but the food in the fridge was still cold. We had a few leftover blocks of C4 from our last mission and put them to good use. That's one home they can't go back to."

"That was incredibly risky," said Trak.

Fitch jumped a mile, not having heard the man behind him at all. All five men stood, their faces pale as they stared at the dark-haired man. As if it were an illusion, his two sons stepped from behind him, grinning.

"Jesus," gasped Ryker, "I'm guessing that makes you Trak Redhawk and sons." Trak said nothing, just staring at the young men.

"It was very risky, but what you did has helped us. Thank you."

"I may need to go change my pants," whispered Bron. His four friends all smiled, then jumped once more as someone tapped their shoulders. Whipping around, Hiro was grinning at them.

"What the ever-loving fuck!" yelled Callahan. "I need to learn to do that."

"You need to know why you're here," said Hiro. "My wife was held by Los Muertos her entire life."

"I'm sure as fuck sorry for that," said Ryker.

"Me too, but all that means is that they cannot get near her now, or ever. You saved us a stop coming back from Belarus, but we'll be destroying the other clubhouse before we return."

"Not necessary," said Ace. "We were able to use the drones to drop explosives on the roof. Made a quick call to the police, and they went out to the location."

"Was anyone hurt?" asked Hiro.

"No. They obviously have access to scanners because they knew the police were coming. The women, those that could move, were put in a van and driven somewhere. Those that couldn't move were left sitting in the parking lot, freezing. Once they were out, I blew the building."

"Fuck, were they hurt at all?" asked Cam.

"Seriously? You're asking me that shit? No, they weren't hurt, but they did have a fire to stay warm until the cops showed up." Hiro just shook his head, laughing.

"They're going to be pissed," said Ghost. "More pissed than they were before. They still have no clue that we have Winter, nor do they know who we are or where we are, but they may do damage to others along the way."

"Then let's get to them before they can do anything else," said Hiro. "Once we hit Miroslav, they'll be running scared. I say we meet them on the road. Ace? Are we following them with the drones?"

"Trying to get their location now," he said. "I'm also still trying to track where they keep their money. They just might be stupid enough to keep it in a pillowcase or some dumb shit like that. If I can find it, I can freeze it."

"Okay, so until then, we take down Miroslav, bring back those two scared little girls, and protect my wife." Hiro looked at the room.

"You know it, brother," said Luke, slapping his back. Cam stepped up once again, taking the last bite of his sandwich.

"Alright, everyone, let's go over this. Plane leaves at 2100."

"2100? But you'll arrive in daylight," said Fitch. Ryan smiled at the men, Thomas now by his side as the engineering and science experts.

"Not on our planes."

CHAPTER TWENTY-THREE

Winter waved one more time as Hiro and the other men left for the planes. She'd never seen him dressed entirely in his black tactical gear. Hiro was always handsome, but for some reason, it made her lady parts tingle, and she wished he had time for another bath.

"It's sexy, isn't it?" smiled Charlie. Winter turned, smiling at the beautiful woman.

"Yes. I didn't think clothes could be sexy or weapons. I mean, I saw the men at Los Muertos carry weapons all the time, and it was never sexy, only scary. I hated it."

"Maybe while the men are gone, Piper, Ani, and Lucia can start your training. It will make you feel more confident and comfortable," said Charlie. "We've all done it."

"I think I might like that," she said. Turning, she noticed that everyone was loading into the SUVs. Her overnight bag had already been taken to the place they called the Sugar Lodge. She saw a few men she'd never seen before and stepped back, standing behind Ghost.

"It's okay, Winter," said the big, older man. "These men are friends. They're all Marines who have taken leave to come and help us, help you."

"Why? Why would they do that? They don't even know me," she asked quietly.

"Winter, there is a brotherhood between servicemen and women. A bond that's almost thicker than blood. We fight together, sleep together, train together, eat together. We have to act as one which is why we hire former military almost exclusively. These men helped Frank when he was bringing Lane home."

"They did?"

"They did, honey," smiled Ghost. "Like all of us, they would never harm you or any woman here. You'll see them, along with the Robicheaux cousins around the property, ensuring that you and everyone here is safe."

"What about you?" she asked innocently. Ghost could only smile.

"Once upon a time, I was a Navy SEAL, Winter. I might be old, but I'm still in great shape and can handle a weapon just fine. Most of the seniors stayed. Nine, Gaspar, myself, Ian, Doc, and Wilson stayed along with Gabriel and Bull. Gaspar's other brothers wanted to go on this mission to have a little exercise." Winter nodded again, smiling up at him.

"Do you have children?" she asked.

"I do," he smiled. "I have two amazing sons who are in the Navy. They both hope to become SEALs one day, and I'm very proud of them."

"I bet you're a good father," she said, looking up at him. "I can tell. I wish I'd had a father like you. Maybe he would have saved me."

"Oh, Winter, I can tell you that if you'd been my daughter, I damn sure would have saved you. Even not as my daughter, I still would have found you and taken you to safety if I had known you were out there. I'm so fucking sorry for everything you had to go through, but sometimes the horrible parts make us better, make us stronger, and you're one of the strongest women I know." She blushed, nodding at him once more.

"I miss Hiro's hugs. Can I hug you?" she asked. Ghost swallowed, giving a nod.

"Yea, honey, you can always give me a hug."

He let her take control of the hug, her thin arms wrapped around his waist, her head lay between his stomach and chest. She was so fucking tiny. He wanted to cry for her. He gently rubbed her back, careful not to squeeze her or make her feel as though she were confined by his embrace. When she pulled back, she smiled at him.

"Thank you," she said. "That was almost as good as Hiro's." She followed the other women to their transportation as Ghost watched.

"Fucking breaks your heart, doesn't it?" said Ian.

"I had boys, not girls, but I'm gonna tell you right now, I hope that son-of-a-bitch tries to come on this property. He deserves to die for what he did to that poor girl. She has this wise, strange insight, yet she's so naïve it's terrifying. Hiro might have the right idea. Lock her up here for the rest of her life so she can be protected."

"We all know that doesn't work," said Gaspar. "But I'm with you. I have six sisters, brother. I had one that was raped, mutilated, beaten. I wanted to hunt that fucker down, and I tried. Believe me, when I got the chance to kill him, I was going to take the chance. Tony just beat us to him. Rachelle finished him off."

"They won't find us, and even if they do, they won't get on the property," said Nine. "All of the fences are now electrified, solar-powered in case they cut the system. They touch those fences; they'll be toast. We just need to make sure everyone is good here until the others return. Let's go."

Winter scanned the grounds as their ATV moved along the muddy path. Despite the fact that the rain had stopped, the moisture-soaked ground was still soft. Pulling through a grouping of thick cypress trees and overgrown brush, she found herself in a beautifully arranged courtyard. There were hanging baskets of flowers, no doubt Mama Irene's touch, benches beneath the covered overhang that once allowed horse and wagon to pull through, and beautifully worked stone paths leading to the lodge.

What you couldn't see was the ten-inch-thick steel plates beneath the walls, allowing the lodge to be nearly impenetrable. Stepping inside, Winter stared at the neatly made cots lining the walls. At the back was a fully functioning kitchen, and on either side of the building were restrooms and showers for men and women.

"It's okay, Winter," said Rachelle. "If you need privacy or quiet, we have a couple of rooms that we use for nursing or medical purposes."

"Oh, I think I'm going to be okay," she said, "but thank you. I was just thinking someone built this because you needed it. More than once."

"Yes, that's right," smiled the other woman. "Their jobs are very dangerous sometimes, and unfortunately, that often places us in potential danger."

"So, I'm not the first one to bring trouble?" she asked.

"You didn't bring trouble," said Gaspar, standing beside his sister. "You did nothing wrong, Winter. We're so very happy that you're here, and I couldn't be happier that you and Hiro found one another."

"He found me," she whispered, looking up at the big man tentatively. "I mean, he found me here, but he found me. The woman I'm supposed to be. Without him, Rachelle, Ashley, Bree, and so many others, I'd still be hiding in my cottage day and night."

"Well, we're damn glad you're not doing that," grinned the big man.

"I bet you're a good dad, too," Winter said, smiling at him. "I haven't met a man here yet that I didn't think would be a good dad."

"I'm always willing to adopt another one, Winter," smiled Gaspar. "Just ask my beautiful wife. We adopted six, and we can always make room for more."

"I might be too old," she grinned, "but thank you. What do we do now? Just wait?"

"Usually," said Rachelle, "we cook, eat, drink, play games, anything to pass the time."

"I'm always hungry," smiled Winter.

"Then that's what we'll do first," smiled Gaspar. "Let's find you some food, and we can put out snacks for everyone."

As the food was set out on the tables, Winter listened to the conversations around her. She knew what all the men did for a living, but hearing the women talk about their work was something she'd not been exposed to on a large scale. Keegan and Tinley she knew about and the medical staff. Learning that there were pilots, engineers, weapons designers, writers, and so much more was mind-blowing for her.

"I always knew I wanted to be a nurse," smiled Ajei. "Besides, once I found out Luke was going to be a SEAL, I figured the training would come in handy."

"Do you have to be really smart to be a nurse?" asked Winter. Ajei gripped the other woman's hand.

"You have to study hard, but you're very smart, Winter. If you wanted to be a nurse, you could do it."

"No," she said, shaking her head. "I don't think I can. I'm not very smart at all. It took me two times to pass my GED."

"Winter," said Dhara, "Jessica, Elizabeth, and I are teachers, and lots of people need two tries to pass their GED. You have to remember that you received no schooling at all until you were almost twenty! I think it's remarkable what you've been able to accomplish."

"Really?"

"Really, sweetie," said Jessica. "If you want, we could start tutoring you, and maybe you could take a few classes online. Is there something that interests you? Nursing? Teaching? Writing?"

"Yes." The women chuckled.

"Which one?" smiled Dhara.

"All of it interests me. I like reading, and I'm really good at it. Is there a job that pays you to read a lot?"

"Actually," smiled Zoe, "I work for a museum curator reviewing items for their value. I look mostly at paintings and sculptures, but there is a specialty in reviewing historical documents and writings."

"Wow," she whispered, "really? I mean, I could sit and read documents all day and say whether they're worth the money?"

"Yes," laughed Zoe, "something like that. If you're interested, I can try to find out what the qualifications are, and then Jessica, Elizabeth, and Dhara can help you choose some college classes."

"You would do that for me?" she asked, surprised.

"Honey, we stick together here, all of us. We mean it when we say we're a family. We help one another out. It's hard when the men are gone, so the women truly rely on one another and work hard to help each other."

"I'll bet you're all great moms," she said with tears in her eyes.

"You'll be a great mom one day, too, Winter," said Elizabeth. "The women you see around you are some of the best examples in the world. They're kind, smart, funny, loving, and giving of themselves like no one I've ever known. My mother wasn't very nice at all, but I was lucky enough to find my way to this family and marry Chris. You'll have the best support team and teachers in the world."

"I'm not glad I had to be at Los Muertos, but I'm glad that I found my way here," smiled Winter. "If the team finds women at their clubhouses, what will happen to them?"

Gaspar and Ghost stood nearby, listening to the conversation. They didn't want to tell her everything, but they needed her to have some knowledge.

"Their clubhouses have been destroyed," said Ghost. "Women were only found in one of them, the one in Nevada. The police took several to local hospitals, but there was a group of women placed in a van and taken somewhere. Do you know where they would take them?"

"He'll want to find a place that's private, somewhere that he can beat the women. He'll blame them for what happened."

"Oh, damn," muttered Code, realizing their mistake.

"Any ideas, Winter? Anything at all that could be helpful," asked Gaspar.

"One of the men, Bones, he was really mean. Not just to me, to all the girls." Nine, Gaspar, Ian, and Ghost stood around her, but the five Marines were now listening as well. "He was the one that would take us to the basement if we had to be punished. He liked it, really liked it. He would laugh the more we cried or begged. He would get excited, down there." She looked toward the crotches of the men around her.

"There was this whip that had these wire pieces at the end. If he didn't whip you with it, he was putting it inside you," she said, staring at the wall.

"Gaspar," whispered Rachelle. He held up his hand, asking his sister for a moment longer.

"When he would whip you with it, he'd sing this song. It was a horrible, terrible song about being a lineman, whatever that is."

"A lineman? *Wichita Lineman*?" asked Ghost.

"Yes, that's it. Wichita. He would laugh and say that's what he was, a Wichita Lineman and that his family would be proud of him."

"Ace!"

"On it," said the man on the other side of the room. Ghost turned, frowning, but didn't have the energy to ask how he'd heard from all the way over there. He turned back to see the pale face of Winter and took a half step forward.

"I don't know about you, Winter," he said softly, "but I could really use a hug right now." Winter looked up at him, her big brown eyes filled with tears. She nodded, then rushed forward, throwing her arms around his waist. He gently held the young woman, rubbing her back.

"It's okay, honey, it's going to be okay. You did nothing wrong. Not a damn thing. You're a survivor, Winter, and that makes you victorious." They must have stayed that way for fifteen minutes, no one moving from her side. When she finally pushed back, she wiped her eyes on her sleeve and smiled up at Ghost.

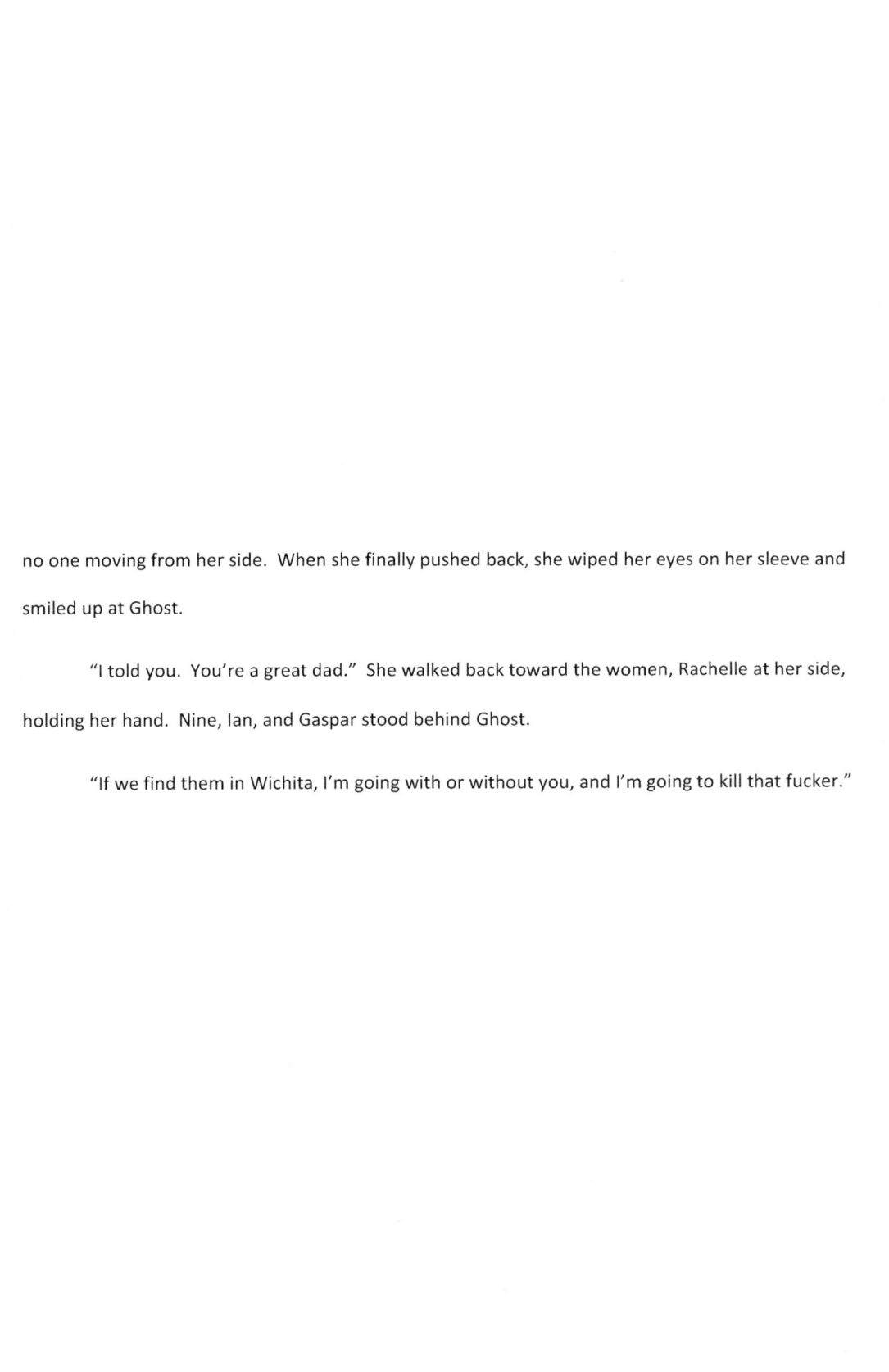

"I told you. You're a great dad." She walked back toward the women, Rachelle at her side, holding her hand. Nine, Ian, and Gaspar stood behind Ghost.

"If we find them in Wichita, I'm going with or without you, and I'm going to kill that fucker."

CHAPTER TWENTY-FOUR

Savannah lowered the Osprey to the snow-covered ground, only a mile from the farmhouse. Bodwick requested to join the team, so he could help to alleviate the fears of the young girls when they were rescued. On his team were Miller, Antoine, Raphael, Parker, Aiden, Titus, Jax, and Fitz.

"You got thirty minutes," she said. "Come back here, and Bodwick will get the girls to safety with Evie. We'll meet Doug and the boys at the mansion. They may need our help."

"Got it," said Miller, nodding. "Be careful."

"Love you, too, brother-in-law," smiled Savannah, blowing her husband a kiss. Raphael winked at her, turning to allow her to take off. Titus sent up the drone, the men all kneeling in the snow. The black sky offered the perfect coverage. He stared at the screen, waiting for the house to come into view, then nodded at the others.

"Two lights on. One in the front of the house, the other at the back."

"Heat signatures?" asked Parker.

"Eight that we can see, but we know that those girls are in the basement, so I probably can't see them. There are three outside watching the perimeter, but they're not doing a very good job of it. One is asleep on the front porch with a cigarette in his hand."

"Dumb shits," muttered Miller. "Let's go. Antoine and Raphael, take the two on the perimeter. Parker, take the one on the porch. The rest of you, get ready to make some loud noises."

Covering the short distance in less than ten minutes, the men kneeled in the nearby field. Using only hand signals, Miller sent his brothers and Parker forward to take the men outside. Watching on their body cameras, Parker stepped up onto the porch, his huge body barely making a sound. When he tapped the man on the shoulder, he swatted at his hand. Tapping him again, he turned as if to rollover and go back to sleep. Parker simply shrugged, ramming his fist into his face. Now on the deck of the porch, he pointed his weapon at the man and fired one bullet into his head, using the silencer. Waiting for the others to signal, he hid on the outside of the door.

Antoine and Raphael listened as the two men at the back of the house spoke in Russian.

"Boss won't let us touch that young pussy," smirked one of the men, "but I need cock sucked. I go to mansion when my shift is over." The other man laughed, nodding. Antoine tapped him on the shoulder. He was so stunned to see someone other than their friend on the other side of the house, he dropped his weapon.

It wouldn't have mattered. Antoine drove his elbow up into his nose, the blood gushing forward as the man fell face-first in the snow, turning the stark white powder a crimson and pink. Raphael admired his brother's work, then turning to the man's shocked partner, shrugged, and fired two bullets into his chest.

"What the fuck?" muttered Antoine. "That didn't take any effort."

"I'm old, not stupid. Save the hand-to-hand for the young boys. Let's go." They signaled the others, waiting to enter the house. Miller took Fitz to the cellar entrance, hoping that his red-haired boyish looks would keep the girls calm until they could get them to Bodwick.

With Antoine, Raphael, and Aiden at the backdoor and Titus, Jax, and Parker at the front, Miller gave a countdown from the cellar door.

"Three, two, one."

Titus and Aiden splintered the old wooden doors easily with one kick. Two men at the kitchen table were doing a line of coke. A bullet stopped them both, putting them face first into their drug of choice. Three men on the sofa were asleep, a porn film playing on the television, their hands tucked in their pants. Jax frowned, a bullet hitting each man in his heart. Titus turned on the heat sensor once more, scanning the floor to see below them. He held up three fingers. Pointing to the corner, he lifted one. Directly below them were two.

As they started to move, they realized the old wooden floors creaked beneath their weight. Antoine frowned, shaking his head. Titus scowled, gently bouncing up and down on the boards. Knowing this was probably going to hurt, he simply bit the bullet and then stepped up onto the kitchen counter. Raphael smiled at him.

"What the fuck are you guys doing?" growled Miller. "It's fucking cold out here." Titus rolled his eyes, Parker, Antoine, and Jax joining him on the countertop. Jax held up three fingers, counting backwards.

When the last finger went down, the four men jumped at the same time, the weathered, termite eaten boards splintering beneath them as they fell through the floor. Jax pointed in the direction of the last guard, firing his weapon three times. He opened the basement door, letting Miller and Fitz inside. Miller looked up at the hole in the ceiling and grinned.

"What the fuck is that?"

"Ingenuity," said Titus. "You're welcome."

"You're American," said one of the girls in the steel cage. Titus turned to see two teenaged girls, naked, and shivering.

"Fuck," muttered Fitz. Lying the back of a chair were two pairs of sweatpants and matching sweatshirts, and he shoved them through the bars. "Put these on until we can find you something better to wear."

"They took our clothes months ago," she said.

"Your fathers told us you were getting weekly calls with them," said Miller.

"No, they filmed those a long time ago. We haven't seen our parents in months. They kept threatening what they were going to do to us, but so far, they've just made us sit in here naked and cold. That one, the one in the corner that you killed, he tried to touch us, but the others kept him away."

"Well, you're going home," said Miller. "Savannah, we have them."

"I'm on way. You need to get to the other house. Chaos is about to break out."

"Anybody wanna tell me why there are so many fucking cars here tonight?" asked Luke.

"Looks like a party," smiled Kiel. "What do you say we join?"

"Eagle, Nathan, Joseph, Hawk, and Ivan, get as high up as you can. Pick off every man that tries to leave. I don't give a shit who he is. We want Miroslav dead or alive. It matters not to me. O'Hara? How many are we looking at inside?"

"So far, I'm counting at least eighty men, probably thirty to forty women," he said with a somber expression. "We need to get into that fucking mansion now. Six men have one woman in a room on the third floor."

"Fuck," muttered Luke. "Alright, teams of five. We've got almost sixty men. We should be able to do this blindfolded. Sharpshooters? Take out the guards on the outside, fast. Uncle Alec, you speak

Russian better than anyone except Ivan. Start walking toward those doors and keep those men engaged until they're dead, then meet us inside. The rest of you, kill those fucking men and get the women out."

"Roger that." Without even saying a word, the men broke off into their five-man teams, crouching low and heading toward the mansion. As they waited for their signal, it came in the form of several distinct, rapid-fire sounds.

Thwap. Thwap. Thwap. Thwap, Thwap, Thwap. Thwap.

"Outside guards are down," said Eagle. "We've got your six, go."

Entering through the back doors, two teams found themselves in the kitchens with a group of extremely frightened kitchen staff. Angel held his finger to his lips and nodded toward the doors. When they didn't move, Alec stepped up and spoke rapidly in Russian.

"Leave now or die." That did it. They ran like they'd just won the lottery.

At the front of the house, Rory led two teams through the front door, dropping several men immediately. Two girls were seated on the sofa, both naked, both clearly underage.

"Go. There are two large limos parked on the street. Get in one." He waited as the wide-eyed girls just stared. "Go!" They ran by him, not caring that it was freezing outside, and they were naked.

"Clear the main floor, then head up," he said, nodding to the others.

On the second floor, Trak, Zeke, Kiel, Cruz, Bryce, Lars, Carter, Carl, Ben, and Liffey entered at the end of the hallway through an open window. Behind the closed doors, they could hear the grunting and groaning of men and the terrified cries of young girls.

Trak and Zeke stared at one another, nodding to the others.

"Take the other end of the hallway," said Trak, his expression dark and menacing. "Noah, Vince, RJ, Eli, and Stone, get up to floor two. You'll need to get the girls out fast."

"Brother..." started Cruz, but Trak simply glared at the man, telling him all he needed to know. As the others moved to the opposite end of the hall, Trak opened the first door. Seeing the young woman bent over a table, her arms and legs tied, she had no option but to suffer through whatever the men wanted to do to her.

She couldn't see her savior, and she damn sure didn't hear him, but neither did the three men who were standing around her tender young body. While two were stroking their own dicks, the third was slapping her bottom as she cried.

Trak slowly withdrew the long buck knife, his steps almost floating toward the offenders. With three quick strokes, the men crumbled to the floors, gasping for air as blood poured from their necks. He cut the girl loose, helping her to stand. Grabbing one of the men's jackets, he draped it around her shoulders and nodded.

"Do you speak English?" she asked.

"Yes," he said quietly. "Go. Downstairs and out the door. A man is there and will help you." She nodded, wiping her tears. Stepping over the three dead bodies, she never even looked down.

Across the hallway, Zeke found two young girls cowering in the corner. Their bottoms were red from spankings, handprints on their tender flesh. Five men smiled at them, all five naked, stroking their bodies to get ready for the ultimate punishment.

Like Trak, he'd chosen knives for this mission, hoping it caused more pain than a bullet to the brain. His serrated blades were designed to tear at the flesh, the victim having no chance at recovery.

With the speed he was born with, he took down one man after another. All five lying on the floor, dying in puddles of their own blood.

Grabbing a blanket from the bed, he held it out to the girls, who stood, wrapping it around their bodies.

"Downstairs," he said. The girls shook their heads. "It's safe. Go downstairs." The older girl, no more than seventeen, shook her head, then signed something at him. He understood ASL, but he was certain this was Russian sign language. Tapping his comms, he waited for their response.

"I need Keith up here, asap. Last room on the right." He just watched the girls, waiting for Keith. When he arrived, he turned, signing to him.

"I think they're deaf, but it's not ASL."

"Are you deaf?" asked Keith. The girls stared at him, signing something that Zeke didn't understand. *"It's Russian. I'll get them downstairs."*

Zeke slapped his back, nodding at the girls as he left. Room to room, he followed his dark brother until their end of the hallway was clear. On the third floor, the others were doing the same. When all the girls were gone, they heard the notice they'd been waiting for.

"I've got Miroslav," said Hiro.

CHAPTER TWENTY-FIVE

"Fucking Americans," said Miroslav. "You can't touch me. No one will touch me. Your federal agents will not allow it." He grinned at the men, his eye already swelling from the first hit landed by Hiro.

"Surprise, surprise," said Hiro. "We're here. We touched you, and you no longer have your leverage."

Miroslav's face turned red, staring at the terrifying group of men standing in front of him. They weren't wearing military uniforms, but that didn't mean they weren't military. Comstock and Whitley promised no one would come or their daughters would die. They knew he would make this happen. How could they be so bold? Did they care nothing for their precious young daughters?

"Your two guests at the farmhouse are on their way home to their parents. The video you so expertly held in your possession is wiped clean. Now that we've cleared that up, tell us about Demon and Los Muertos."

Miroslav looked at the faces once again, wondering how they could connect him to the American biker. Their agreement had been long-standing. Demon found the women, prepared them for his use, and he paid him handsomely.

"Nothing to tell," he shrugged. "You know this man. You know what he does. End of story as you say."

"No," said Hiro, stepping forward. He gripped Miroslav's neck, the blood draining from his face. His eyes bulged, sweat pouring down his face. "It's not the end of the story. That blackhearted bastard raped and beat my wife. I want to know why. Why would he do that to his own child?" Releasing his grip, the man sagged forward, coughing, and spitting blood.

"I really need to learn to do that," smiled Dalton.

"Why?" asked Hiro, staring at the choking Miroslav.

"He has no child," said Miroslav.

"Yes, he does."

"No. His son died. Long time now." Hiro frowned, wondering why the man would lie about this.

"He has a daughter. Blonde hair and brown eyes." Miroslav shook his head.

"No. Is his granddaughter. His son left the club without permission, ran away, and married nice girl far away. Had a good life. Demon tracked him down and killed him. Wife was gone from house, but she had no one to help her. Parents would give her nothing. The wife had no option but to go to him for help. She was foolish to think he would be kind because of child. Blonde girl is his granddaughter. He was getting her ready to send to me."

Hiro turned his back to the man, then whipping his left leg around, caught him on the side of the head, his neck snapping to the side.

"She won't be coming to you or to anyone," said Hiro. "She is my wife."

"Wife," said Miroslav, waving him off. "Is joke. Girl can't be wife. Belongs to Demon. She is broken."

"No, she is not broken. She is perfect and beautiful and mine. All mine." Hiro took two steps back this time, staring at the man. "You're going to die now, and my face will be the last you ever see." He lifted one knee, then as quickly, lowered it and rushed forward, his right leg slamming into the other man's head, his left flying sideways across his face. The sickening crunch of bones told everyone in the room that Miroslav was dead.

"The girls are in the limos and being taken to hospitals," said Kiel. "What do you want to do, Hiro?"

"I want to burn this fucking place to the ground and then go home and see my wife before I track that bastard down and break every bone in his body."

Standing on the lawn of the mansion, the men watched as the orange glow of fire lit up the night sky. The dead bodies inside the mansion would keep investigators busy for months, but Hiro didn't care. Dozens of girls were free. Perverts were dead, and Miroslav would never sell another body or bag of drugs again.

He felt a strong hand at his shoulder and looked up to see Alec.

"Let's go home, Hiro."

CHAPTER TWENTY-SIX

"I think I've found them," said Ace, walking toward the seniors. "I had to try and find out the real name of the man that Winter spoke to us about. It wasn't easy…"

"Ace? Get to it, brother." Ghost stared at him, his arms folded across his chest.

"Do you guys have any fucking clue how hard this shit is?" Nine and Gaspar laughed. "What? What's so funny?"

"Nothing, just that Sly, Code, and Pigsty have been telling us that for years. Problem is, brother, you boys make it look too easy."

"Whatever," frowned Ace. "You're going to listen whether you like it or not. Bones didn't travel far from his real name. Arthur Joseph Bone served twenty-five years for murdering his parents, two sisters, and older brother. The only reason he wasn't given longer was that he was sentenced as a minor. His father owned a large granary and farm supply center serving most of the Midwest. Apparently, Bones was a problem child as early as kindergarten, hurting animals, bullying other children, even attacking teachers here and there.

"The family-owned Victorian mansion is one of the largest in the state. Everyone knew who the Bone family was. On the night of the murders, Arthur bragged to his good buddy that he was about to have some fun. When the friend asked what he was going to do, he said, and I quote, 'fuck my sisters.' At first, his friend didn't think anything of it, but the more he thought about it, he realized he might be telling the truth.

"By the time the sheriff's department arrived, his mother and father were hanging in the attic, his brother was nailed to the front of the barn door, and his sisters were raped, mutilated, and tied to their beds. They found our friend Bones eating a bowl of cereal in the kitchen. He didn't deny anything, didn't ask for a lawyer, just outright said 'I did it.'

"When the police interviewed his friend, showing him the pictures, they were struck by the fact that his good buddy, although he'd called the Sheriff on him, wasn't horrified or bothered by the pictures."

"Ace, tell me this fucking story ends soon," growled Ghost.

"Fine. Old grumpy asshole. Yes, it ends soon. His friend was Demon, better known as Warren Joseph Bell, Jr."

"Jesus, he became a copycat?" asked Gaspar.

"No. It seems that Warren was the original. He just didn't want his friend doing what he wanted to be doing, at least not without him. Warren had been raping and brutalizing women since he was fifteen through the club, but no one knew that except Bone. He thought it was cool and got a little taste for it a few years later. Warren matured, unfortunately, and realized he could use his friend's tastes to further his own. That Victorian mansion is still standing, still owned by him.

"I asked the authorities to do a drive-by, and sure enough, there are forty or fifty motorcycles in front of the place. They didn't have any problems at all backing away. He said they don't have the manpower to do a damn thing about it. They could call in the state, but it will take a while. I asked him to leave it alone. We had someone who would handle it." Ace waited, staring at the seniors, their new friends now joining the group as well.

"The cousins have the exterior, sir," said Fitch. "We'd be happy to go with you, but for the sake of the brotherhood, I know that Hiro wants Demon, and I have to guess he'll want the other one as well."

Nine stared at the five young Marines. They were well trained, disciplined, young, but also on active duty.

"If you get caught out there, you risk your careers," said Nine.

"We're aware, sir."

"No fucking sirs," he growled. "Jesus, I'm already a grandfather and fucking ancient. Just Nine."

"Got it," grinned the younger man. "We know this could come back on us, and we're all willing to take the chance for that girl. She deserves closure so that she can live a normal life. Bron and I are retiring in forty-nine days, six hours, and twelve minutes. Give or take. We're good." He looked at the other men and waited for them to respond.

"It's all good, s- uh, Nine. We're three to four years from our retirement, but we'll trust that if we get nailed to the wall, you'll send a cake with a file in it."

"Fucking right we will," grinned Ian. "Alright, the nine of us to Wichita."

"You're not fucking going without me," said Wilson, striding toward the men.

"Or me," said Doc.

"Come on, boys," smiled Molly, "you're gonna need a lady to fly you up there. Besides, I'd like a piece of those animals myself."

"Molly, what about Asia?"

"She's good with it, just this time. One thing we don't tolerate well is men hurting women. Gabriel and Bull are here as well, and both want to come. They went to grab some of the weapons from the office."

"Are we leaving the women vulnerable?" asked Gaspar.

"I can't believe you just said that," said Matthew.

"Does everyone hear every fucking conversation in this place?" asked Gaspar. Matthew grinned, glancing over his shoulder at Martha.

"Remy and Robbie are headed back here now to guard the lodge. Between your Mama, George, and Mary, we'll be just fine. The other cousins are still out there on the property, and we have all five dogs plus the ones that are almost fully trained. If your flying camera thing says all those motorcycles are at that house, then they don't know where you are and where she is. You go get those two men. Do what you need to do to the rest but bring those two back and let Hiro have his justice. We'll be just fine here."

"Pops," started Gaspar.

"Gaspar, you forget that I served as well. I understand, son. Take those two men to the old mansion on the island. We'll be just fine."

Gaspar looked at Nine, Ian, and Ghost, their looks telling him what he needed to know. He nodded, turning toward Fitch, Callahan, Ryker, Justice, and Bron.

"Alright, gather everything we might need. Any of you boys handy with explosives?"

"Oh! Me! Me!" said Ryker, jumping up and down.

"Like a fucking child," growled Ghost. "Reminds me of Trevor." Ian nodded, then spoke to the five Marines.

"Gather your shit and meet us downstairs. You're about to have your audition."

"They found them," said Miller, staring at Hiro. He was leaning back in his seat on the plane, his eyes closed, trying to get some sleep. Slowly, he opened his eyes. "They're in Wichita. The seniors, and a few others, are going up to wipe them out, except Demon and the other dude."

"Thank you," said Hiro, nodding his head.

"We know what it's like, brother. We'll meet them on the old mansion island. The land has been expanded so there's a spot for us to land out there if we need to. For now, get some sleep. I'll keep you up-to-date if we know anything before we land."

Hiro let out a slow breath, relaxing his body as he tried to calm his speeding heart. There were so many things racing through his head, so many thoughts on how to torture these men. He had the ability to kill them with his bare hands or with weapons. There was also a sick desire to give them the same pain they'd given his beautiful wife.

"Hey, Hiro?" said Axel, gripping his forearm. "Don't take this on alone, brother. We're all here to support you. You get the kill, but we'll be there to do whatever you want. Understand?"

"I understand. Thank you," he said, sitting up and realizing that all eyes were on him. "Thank you all. I keep thinking that Winter might want to say something to them, to see them, but I don't want to put her through that."

"We could ask Pops," said Antoine. "If she wants to be out there, he can bring her out there."

"Let's wait to see if they get the two of them," he said.

"I think they'd be seriously fucking pissed if they heard you say that. They will get them, Hiro. The seniors might be old as fuck, but they're still big, badass, and strong as shit. The Marines are going with them, as well as Molly, Doc, Wilson, Bull, and Gabriel."

"Didn't mean to offend anyone," he grinned. "I just want to make it right for her, you know. I want her to be able to walk around and not fear that her own fucking grandfather is going to take her and abuse her. It's taken us months to get her to where she is now. I don't want anything to set her back."

Miller watched the young man wrestling with something deep inside and looked at his brothers, their faces telling him that they saw the same thing.

"Hiro? What's really bothering you?" Hiro looked at the men, then looked down at his lap.

"You're going to think it's stupid. I keep wondering. I mean, my parents always believed in karma. I killed those men that killed my grandfather. Maybe this is my karma."

"Fucking bullshit," growled Jean. "No offense, Hiro, but that's not how that shit works. You removed a group of men from this planet that deserved to die. There's no backlash on that. If there were, we'd all be dead. This is nothing but the universe pulling its fucking games again.

"We've all been where you are, Hiro. Between Marie, Cait, Rachelle, Alexandra, hell a dozen more, we know what it's like to want to kill the man or men that hurt the woman you love. What you're experiencing right now? It's what happens when you're a true RP man, brother."

"Welcome to the fucking club," smirked Axel.

"What about all those girls? The ones we stuck in the limos?"

"They were all taken to local hospitals. About half were American. The embassy will make sure they get home. We contacted Comstock and Whitlow to let them know that Evie was on her way with their daughters. She's another one that suffered in her past, Hiro. She's the perfect person to talk to those two young women, although she says they're both doing surprisingly well considering what they went through."

"They were very lucky," he nodded.

"Fucking big lucky," said Max, walking toward the group. "Code just sent word that when the Belarussians arrived at the fire, they discovered a mass grave site behind the mansion. It's estimated there are more than two hundred bodies back there, all women. Turns out the mansion didn't belong to Milosevic. It belonged to a high-ranking female in the Belarus government. I'm sure more heads will fall from that one."

"Jesus," muttered Hiro. Miller slapped the young man's knee, standing to head back to his own seat.

"This isn't karma, Hiro. What's about to be delivered is justice."

CHAPTER TWENTY-SEVEN

Sly and Code traveled with the Wichita team, concerned for their safety and their abilities to manage the plethora of technology they now used. Not only were half of them over the age of sixty, but there were five men who'd never worked with them before. Someone had to keep their head on straight.

Molly lowered the Osprey in the field. Her whisper technology sounded like a heavy breeze. There was snow on the ground, so in all likelihood, Demon and his men would be nestled inside by a fire.

"Ryker? Set the charges to blow the house to ashes. Ghost? Disable every fucking bike out there," said Nine.

"Man, this is gonna be so much fun," grinned the older man.

"Hey, it is gonna be fun, but let's not forget that it's dangerous as well. These assholes are reckless and psychotic. They'll shoot first and won't care who they're shooting at. Let's use our experience to nail them down." Nine turned to the seniors. "Ghost, once you get those bikes disabled, send them tumbling. If I know a biker, he'll come running to save his baby."

"And if I know a narcissistic psychopath, he'll stay inside safe and sound," said Gaspar. "Code? What are the heat signatures?"

"Doesn't look like any women. They all seem to be just lying around the house. We were right. There are about forty-one, two… maybe fifty-five inside."

"That matches the bike count," said Ghost.

"Alright, let's get this shit done," growled Nine.

Ghost nodded, making his way toward the bikes with Bron. While he disabled each of the bikes, Bron watched his back, making sure no one came from the house. There were no lights on the outside and only a few flickering lights on the inside, so they most likely only had candle power.

"This is taking too long," said Bron. He pulled his knife and began walking down the rows of bikes, slashing the tires. Ghost looked at him, rolling his eyes, as he continued to cut the wires. "Done."

"Done," smirked Ghost. "Ready?"

"Ready," said Bron, bracing his body against the frame of the first bike. With a hard thrust, the two men pushed the first bike in their row over, then watched as they fell like dominoes. When they got to the fourth row, they could hear men rustling inside.

"Take cover!" whispered Ghost.

The two men ran toward a burnt-out van, hiding behind the shell. On the roof of the house, they saw the drones dropping explosives while Ryker set charges lower. Wilson and Doc jammed the locks on the front and back doors when it appeared the last man had run toward the bikes. Carefully sneaking off the front porch, Doc ran to the side where Wilson waited for him.

"Kill 'em all," said Nine.

Using their night vision goggles and night scopes, the men lay flat in the fields, firing on the unsuspecting, drug and alcohol confused bikers. Several pulled their weapons, but were firing blindly, not able to hit anything. A few tried to run, but Justice, using a long-range sniper rifle, easily picked them off.

Wilson heard someone attempting to get out of the house, driving their body against the jammed door. At the back of the house, a few moments later, they tried again.

"What now?" asked Bron.

"Now, you learn patience, grasshopper," smiled Ian. The younger man looked at him, frowning, confusion on his face.

"Grasshopper? What does that mean?"

"Seriously," he said, looking at the young Marine. "Christ, I'm fucking old."

They knew that it was most likely Demon and Bones inside the house, but they needed to be sure. What they were positive of is that they had nothing more than a few handguns at best.

"Hey," said Ryker, "everything is ready to blow, and in case you wanted to know, there were five suitcases of drugs in the shed out back. I rigged that as well." Ian grinned at the young man and nodded.

"Nice work, Marine."

"What the fuck do you want?" yelled the voice from inside the house.

"We just want to have a friendly chat," said Nine.

"Who the hell are you? What beef do you have with me? You killed all my fucking men!"

"Yea, I did do that," he smirked. "But then again, you rape and beat children, kill them when you're done, so I'd say I did the world a favor. In fact, I did your granddaughter a huge favor."

Silence met his statement, and he heard the banging on the door once again. Desperate to get out, Demon fired his pistol at the lock on the door, finally pushing it open far enough to get out. Stumbling onto the porch, he waved the handgun in the air.

"Where is she? Where is Girl?"

"She has a name fuck-wad. You're a really special kind of sick twisted bastard, aren't you? Your buddy with you? You in there, Bones?"

"How the hell do you know my name?" yelled the man on the inside of the house.

"Oh, we know a lot about you boys. We know about the pit of bodies in Colorado. We know that your houses in Nevada and Arizona went boom. We know that you've been looking for the child for years now. And we know that your sick, sorry, pathetic asses won't ever make it to a jail cell."

"I'm right here," yelled Demon, "shoot me if you have the guts!"

"Please," said Ghost, "can I?"

"Alright, just this once, but only in the leg or arm," said Gaspar in a playful tone. Ghost smiled, lining up his scope and hitting Demon in the upper thigh, narrowly missing the artery.

"Ahhh!" he screamed, falling to the porch. "Bones! Bones, get out here, and fucking help me."

"Help yourself! I ain't gettin' killed."

"Well, see, that's where you're wrong," said Gaspar. "The whole house is rigged to blow. You've got yourself about twenty-five seconds to walk toward us, or you're going to be in little bitty pieces."

"You're bluffing!" he yelled. Gaspar turned to Ryker.

"Blow the shed."

He jumped up and down, the detonator in his hand. The young man reminded him of his brother, Miller. An explosives expert, he loved nothing more than to make things go boom. The shed exploded into slivers of aluminum, the drugs going with them. They heard the expletives flying from the two men, then the shadowy figure of Bones stepping up next to his friend.

"Walk toward us," said Gaspar. "Keep your hands up, and you better hope to fuck you don't have any weapons on you."

"Code?" said Nine. "Scan them."

"Knife in Bones' left boot, pistol at Demon's back."

"Stop!" yelled Nine. "Bones, you mind throwing that knife in your boot across the field? Demon, same with the pistol at your back. Now."

He heard one of them mutter 'shit,' but watched as the knife was thrown and the pistol followed.

"Nothing detected now," said Code.

"Keep walking," yelled Gaspar.

When the men were twenty feet from them, he turned and nodded to Ryker, who hit the detonator for the house. The shards of wood flew fifty feet in the air, the old home reduced to a pile of burning rubble.

"Kneel," said Callahan, pointing his rifle at the men. They stared at the younger man, their faces in defiance. "I said kneel motherfucker, or I will blow your brains all over this field."

Both men kneeled, grunting as they did. Justice patted them down, then secured their hands with zip ties.

"We ain't gonna do no time," said Demon. "Feds won't let that happen."

"You're out of fucking luck," said Gabriel. "The Comstock and Whitlow girls are already home, safe and sound. Your buddy, Milosevic, is dead, and so are almost a hundred men who decided to party at the mansion last night."

"You're lyin'," said Demon.

"I don't lie, you asshole. You're fucking dust. You just don't know it yet."

"Where's Girl?"

"Now see, that pisses me off," said Ghost, stepping closer to the man. He slammed his fist into his jaw, the man falling back in the snow. "Remember, asshole, I don't give a fuck if you die. No one does. Well, that's not true. Someone wants you alive for a hot minute anyway. Your granddaughter is married, happily."

"No! She's mine! I get to do what I want with her. I got the right," he yelled.

"You have no fucking rights," growled Gaspar, gripping the man's shirt and lifting him to his feet. "You lost all rights the day you became a sick, twisted degenerate. I would carve you into little pieces, but I made a promise to let someone else do it, and I'll damn sure keep it. Wilson? Doc? Let these animals get some sleep."

The needles were jammed into their necks, both men falling over against the hard-packed snow. They were so filled with other drugs, Doc and Wilson made sure that there was more than enough to knock them out for the flight to the island.

"Shit, these guys stink," said Ryker, bending down to lift Demon.

"Well," smiled Nine, "grab his ankles and drag him through the snow. That might clean him up a bit for his interview with his judge."

Two men took an ankle for each man, dragging their bodies toward Molly and the bird. Their heads were bouncing off the hard earth, hitting rocks, ice, and everything else along the way. Zip tying their ankles, they connected the ties at their backs, effectively hog tying both men as they tossed their bodies into the helicopter.

When they landed on the old mansion island, Gaspar and Ghost took the small boat that was tied at the dock, heading back to Belle Fleur. The team would be back any time now, and someone needed to tell Winter. Just as they got into the ATV, the SUVs began pulling onto the property.

"Everybody good?" asked Nine. Hiro nodded.

"Where are they?"

"They're out at the old mansion island. We were just going to see Winter. She needs to know, Hiro," said Gaspar.

He nodded, sitting in the back of the big ATV as the seniors headed to the lodge. When they opened the doors, everyone was already up and eating breakfast. Winter saw Hiro and ran toward him, launching herself into his arms.

"Hi, baby," he said with a pain-filled smile.

"I missed you," she said, kissing him. She pulled back, staring at his face. "What's wrong? What did I do wrong?"

"Honey, you did nothing wrong, nothing. You're perfect, Winter, so fucking perfect," he said, hugging her close once again. "I need you to hear what we all have to say, okay?" She nodded.

"You know that we went to get the girls back, and we did. We saved several women, in fact."

"That's good," she smiled.

"Yes, that's very good, but while we were there, Nine and the others went to Wichita and found Demon and Bones." She looked at the older men, landing on Ghost's face.

"Did you kill them?" she asked, staring at him.

"No, honey, we didn't kill them yet. Hiro should be the one that gets to kill them. Or…"

"Or you," said Hiro. She stepped back from the men, shaking her head.

"I-I can't kill anyone. I can't. I hate them. I want them dead, but I don't think I can kill them. I've thought about it a million times. I've dreamed of being able to do it, but I don't think I can."

"It's okay, baby, you don't have to do anything. You don't have to see them. We're going to take care of this. I just wanted you to know." She nodded, biting her lower lip.

"Is it wrong of me to want them dead? I'm putting the burden on all of you, and that's not right," her eyes filled with sadness and love for the people around her.

"No," said Ghost, stepping forward. "Not in the least. This is what we do, Winter. It's our jobs, getting rid of the bad guys."

"Are you going to make me leave once they're gone?" she looked at Hiro, then back at Ghost. "Will you all make me go away when this is done?"

"Winter, you're not going anywhere, honey," said Ghost, stepping forward. Hiro nodded at the older man, knowing that she needed to hear from someone other than her husband that all would be well. "You are part of this family, sweetie. You belong here, with Hiro as his wife, but with all of us. Hell, you heard Gaspar earlier. He'll adopt you if you want." She let out a nervous laugh, wiping the tears away.

"You'll come back to me?" she asked Hiro. "We have to finish the boat for Mardi Gras. It's in three days."

"Baby, I will be back very soon, and we will damn sure finish that boat. Let me handle this for both us, and then we're going to really start living our lives. Maybe even take a honeymoon somewhere. What do you think about that?" he said, holding her hands.

"Could we go to Disneyland?" The men all chuckled, nodding their heads.

"I think that sounds perfect," said Hiro. "Winter? Do you know who Demon really is? Who he is to you?"

She stared at Hiro, fear passing over her face once again, and he could have kicked himself. He didn't want her to fear this. He wanted her to feel safe knowing that he understood.

"He always said I was his, that I belonged to him. He would call me stupid, all kinds of horrible names, but I saw a picture in his room once. It was of his son. If my hair were still blonde, I would look just like him." She looked at Hiro and the other men, waiting to see if they would say anything. "Is he my father? Did my own father do this to me?"

"No, baby, he's not your father. His son was your father. Demon is your grandfather, although he damn sure doesn't deserve that title."

"My grandfather," she whispered, shaking her head. She looked at Gaspar and Nine. "You're grandfathers. You would never do this, would you?"

"No, honey, we would never do anything like this. He's not normal, Winter. His head isn't right. You're not like him, and you'll never be like him. You are a good person," said Gaspar. She turned to look at Hiro.

"Don't you hate me for this? My grandfather touched me. He beat me and did things to…"

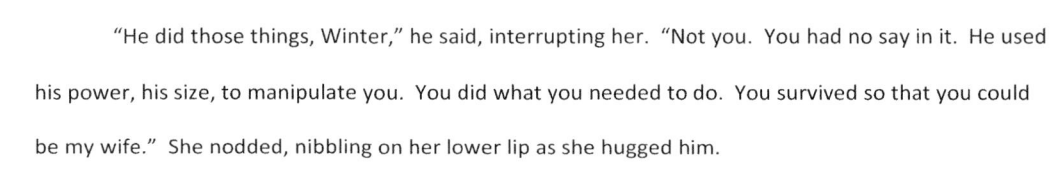

"He did those things, Winter," he said, interrupting her. "Not you. You had no say in it. He used his power, his size, to manipulate you. You did what you needed to do. You survived so that you could be my wife." She nodded, nibbling on her lower lip as she hugged him.

"I love you," she said, kissing him.

"I love you, too, baby." He kissed her sweetly, then pulled her in for a deeper, more amorous kiss. "I'll be back." She nodded, giving him a sweet smile.

"I'll be waiting."

CHAPTER TWENTY-EIGHT

Demon opened his eyes to the blinding light of sunshine beating down on his face. The banging on the inside of his head was nearly more than he could stand. He tried to remember why he had such a hangover but failed to recall the evening before. All he knew was that his skull felt as though it were being crushed from the inside out.

Trying to move, he found himself restrained and looked to his left to see that Bones was staring straight ahead. He followed the man's eyes and knew why his friend looked frightened. Demon saw his fair share of big men in his day, but these men were in another class. They were big in every variety. Wide, tall, muscular, more muscular. The wall of muscle was intimidating even for a man who claimed he never felt fear.

"This a fucking party," he growled, trying to act as though he weren't fazed by it all.

"It is," said Hiro, "it's a funeral. Yours and your psycho sidekick's, to be exact."

"Pftt," said Demon, jerking his head, "whatever you say, Chinaman."

"Really? You fucking people are something else." Hiro shook his head, the soft chuckles behind him infuriating the two men seated on the wet grass. "As I told your buddy in the bar, I'm Japanese, so get it fucking straight. And you may want to give me a little respect. I am, after all, your grandson-in-law."

Demon tried to get off the ground, the wet earth making it difficult. The spongy ground forcing his body to slide back, never able to get his legs under him.

"There's a piece of me that wants desperately to just carve you into little pieces and feed you to the alligators, but that could, quite possibly, contaminate the gator population for generations to come.

I mean, I'm a nature guy all the way, and what did those poor gators ever do to me? There's another side of me that just wants to cut you loose and kill you with my bare hands, and believe me, I can."

"So do it, Chinaman," he chided. He stared at the younger man and knew that if he married Girl, he would be easily egged on. "She's a sweet piece of ass, isn't she? I sure enjoyed her, just like I enjoyed her mama before I killed the bitch. My fucking boy left me, left the club. My own flesh and blood walked out on me; can you imagine? He was all pissed because he didn't think we were doin' things the right way. Thought he could run from me.

"He went and got that girl pregnant and married her. Stupid fuck. I made sure his dead body was never found. That little cunt didn't have a choice but to come to me for help after I had a little talk with her folks. Yea, I told 'em all about what their sweet little girl would be doin' in my club. She came runnin' to me for help. I gave her some help. Fucked her with that ripe belly until my Girl was born. Then fucked her a few hours later. The blood turned me on."

Hiro connected with his jaw, the roundhouse kick sending him to the damp earth again. When he was finally able to catch his breath once more, the older man pushed up on his elbows, finally able to sit again.

"Yea, Girl made me hard, woo-eee," he grinned. "Let the boys fuck her too. Yes sirree, they did her good."

"Hiro, you kill this fucker, or I will," said Alec, stepping up, cracking his knuckles. Bones and Demon looked up and up and up, staring at the goliath before them.

"Just trying to let him dig his grave. I want to be sure there is no doubt in my mind how I justify tearing his body apart." Demon sneered at Hiro, then stared up at Alec, wanting to provoke the big man.

"Whatsa matter, big boy? Don't like hearin' about..."

"Shut up," said the small voice behind them all. Hiro turned, wide-eyed to see Winter standing next to Mama Irene. Her huge eyes were wide with fear but also filled with a courage and determination that Hiro didn't expect to see. Her dark hair was pulled up on top of her head, her cheeks red from the wind of the boat ride.

"What'd you say, Girl?" growled Demon, believing he still held power over her.

"I said," she took a step toward him, "shut up. You will not speak to my friends and family or my husband that way. You will not speak to anyone ever again. I lived through hell because of you, because of your sick, twisted mind. All of you. All of you deserve to die. You are broken. Broken in more ways than anyone could ever know."

"Girl, you best watch what you..."

"Shut up!" she screamed. "Shut up! I survived. Me! The girl you called stupid. Well, guess what, Demon, I'm not stupid. I have a career, a husband, friends, and I'll be getting a college diploma. And you, you will never breathe life on this planet again.

"I will not listen to you any longer. I will not look at you any longer. I have dreamed every night of doing this. Every night since I can remember, since I was old enough to have such dreams. Now, they are replaced with happy dreams because of my husband. I am done."

The grin on his face said that he didn't believe she would do anything, but that grin was replaced with shock when Winter pulled a pistol from the back of her jeans.

"Winter..." started Hiro.

The gun fired six times, then she pointed it at a shocked, blood-splattered Bones and fired four more times. Her shots weren't exactly accurate, but they didn't have to be at close range and with a nine-millimeter. Irene stepped up and took the gun from her hand, kissing her cheek.

"Let me have that, child," she said gently. She turned, handing the gun to Alec. "Clean that and put it back in my nightstand. You know where it goes. Make sure it's fully loaded again."

"Yes, Mama," smiled Alec.

"Winter?" Hiro reached for her hand, pulling her toward him. "Honey, I was going to take care of it. I didn't want you to see him, to hear what he was saying."

"I know, but I needed to do it. The longer you were gone, the more I realized that I needed to finish this, for me. He was goading you to let him loose so that he could fight you one on one. I know that you would have beaten him, but you might have been hurt in the process, and I couldn't stand that. I didn't want him to hurt anyone ever again. Are you angry?"

"No, honey, I'm not angry. I'm so damn proud of you," he said, kissing her.

"Me too," said Ghost. Winter turned to him and smiled.

"Like a father would be?" she said with a frightened grin.

"Exactly like a father would be, Winter. Exactly."

"You got yourself a whole bunch of fathers now, Winter," smiled Gaspar. "I told you that I'd adopt you, but I think we've decided that you're adopted by all of us now. Hiro better not step out of line, or he'll have all of us to answer to."

"Let's go back to the cottage, honey. I think we have a lot to talk about, and I want to make sure you're doing alright."

"What about them? They shouldn't be buried on this beautiful property. They don't deserve it," she said, staring at Demon.

She took a step closer, staring down at her tormentor of nineteen years. A man who should have been protecting her instead making her life hell. They watched it bubbling to the surface, then she screamed. It was ear-piercing, shrill. She kicked his dead body over and over again, her tiny body barely causing any damage, but it didn't matter. She was letting go of the hate and anger.

Hiro just watched her, tears rolling down his face, letting her get this out. He turned to ask Gaspar how long he should let her do this when he noticed that all the men were crying. It was Ghost who finally stepped forward, wrapping his arms around her small body from behind. He lifted her, turning her in his arms and just holding her.

"It's done, honey. It's done. He can't hurt you or anyone ever again. You are so damn brave, Winter, so fucking brave. I'm so proud of you," he whispered. Winter sobbed into his big chest, her feet dangling in the air. "There, there, it's alright now. You can live, Winter."

"He's right, child," said Irene. "You can live your life now, with your husband." Ghost set her on the ground, his big hands wiping the tears from her face. He smiled at her, giving her a kiss on her forehead.

"I wish I'd known you my whole life," she said in a shuddering breath.

"Your life begins now, Winter. Just take a step forward." She turned to see Hiro crying, his face blotchy and red.

"Okay. We move forward," she said, taking one last look at Ghost. "I don't feel anything. Should I feel anything?"

"Not a damn thing, sweetie."

It would be a few days, but Winter eventually did feel a myriad of emotions. She cried. She got angry. She threw a few things at Hiro's head. She even went for a run. When it was over, she spent two hours in a therapy session with Ashley and came out feeling like a new woman, the woman she was always meant to be.

Mama Irene offered to place a headstone for her parents in the family plot, but Winter said no. She didn't know them in life. Visiting them in death wouldn't help her.

When they unveiled the Mardi Gras boat, everyone gasped at the beautiful job they'd done. The streamers, masks, beads, and colorful lights reflected off the bayou. On the upper deck were king and queen chairs waiting for Frank and Lane.

"Winter, I can't thank you enough for making my wish come true," said Frank. "I can announce to the whole world that not only is Lane queen of the Robicheaux Krewe, but she's my wife as well. May I hug you?"

"I think I'd like that," she said, nodding. Frank gave her a small hug at first, but when she tightened her grip around his waist, he laughed, hugging her more fiercely.

Down by the dock, there were dozens of chairs and blankets lining the shore, watching as the floats passed, throwing beads and candy. Winter had never seen anything so wonderful in all her life. She cheered and yelled, waving at all the parade-goers. Hiro thought it might be the most perfect moment ever.

When their boat passed, they noticed the big sign on the front 'Winner – Best on the Bayou.'

"What does that mean?" she asked, looking around. Irene smiled at her, clapping her hands.

"That means your boat was the best of the entire fleet, sweetie. You won, Winter. You won." Cheers erupted, and for the first time in her life, she laughed when they rose above the trees, caressing her body in a way that said 'you are loved.' Turning in Hiro's arms, she whispered to him.

"We won, right, Hiro?"

"Absolutely, baby, we won."

CHAPTER TWENTY-NINE

The addition of Thomas to G.R.I.P. was resulting in some fast-moving new projects that had them all wondering if they could keep up with the egghead. When he started discussing some advancements in the tracking devices that could deliver biometric information, he caught Hiro out of the corner of his eye and knew he needed to let the world know.

"If we connect the tracking devices to the blood supply, we can provide greater data to home base while we're in the field," he said.

"Won't that interfere in the ability to fight infection?" asked Hiro. The room narrowed their gaze as he spoke.

"That's right," said Thomas. "What do you suggest?"

"I-I don't know. I mean, maybe something a little less invasive or less likely to stop working. If someone was killed, we would still want to locate their body, so don't attach it to a vital organ. I would think hiding it behind the ear is the better way to do that. It might even be possible to help in the case of a head injury or equilibrium issues."

"And just how in the fuck do you know all that?" asked Dom.

"Oh, well..."

"Well?" asked Luke staring at him. Hiro blushed, looking down at his feet. "We said total transparency and honesty, Hiro. You found a way to hide your medal. What's this all about?"

"If you don't mind," said Thomas. "My apologies, Hiro. I did that intentionally, and he knows that I did. While Hiro was working on his degrees in the military, he was able to take an advanced master's curriculum at the university where I was teaching. It should have taken a year. Hiro finished it in four months. With a perfect grade. I encouraged him to continue toward his PhD, but he was re-deployed and wasn't able to do it virtually. We never met face-to-face, but when I learned of his name after my rescue, well, I knew I needed to work with him."

"Hiro? Again, why would you hide that from us?" asked Cam.

"Some of you understand this, but I've been defined by the way I look for my entire life. You're Asian. You should be smart and know martial arts. My father was right about that. I played into the stereotype and became proficient at all the things the world said I should be proficient in. I wanted to be defined by my good deeds, not my abilities."

"But they're one and the same, Hiro," said Eric. "You do good deeds because of your body and your brain, your abilities. It's connected, brother."

"I'm sorry," he said, shaking his head. "I promise, that's all the secrets I have."

"Nope," said Cam. "Out with it. How many languages do you speak? What's your IQ?" The entire room smirked at the man squirming in front of them.

"Eight. One-seventy-one." Whistles and catcalls followed, joking with him.

"Are you interested in working out at G.R.I.P. half of the time?" asked Cam. He and Thomas had already spoken, and Thomas felt like Hiro could be a valuable asset to the group at G.R.I.P. but also knew the man wanted to participate in missions.

"Just half, right?" Cam nodded. "Then, yes. I'd love to do that."

"Good, then Grandma's celebration lunch won't be wasted," smiled Luke. "Let's go, boys, crawfish and crab boil, food and music, and a celebration for Hiro and Winter."

As the men filed out of the room, laughing and joking, Zeke gripped Dom's shoulder, pulling him to the side.

"Have you seen the news this morning?" asked Zeke.

"No, I try to avoid all the happy shit happening in the world," said Dom.

"You might want to look up a story on your phone. The girl from the diner in California, the ex-actress, Livvi Downs…"

"Leightyn, her name is really Leightyn."

"Yea, her. The producer that fucked her over released all these nude photos of her over the internet. Poor girl can't make a move without the paparazzi following her, trying to film her. She's also got a few sicko stalkers now."

"Fucking hell," muttered Dom.

"Yea. One of the entertainment shows said everyone knows that the photos were taken illegally. You can see that she was in her bedroom or dressing room in every one of them. It was also revealed that the producer and her agent were the ones that blackballed her together. The agent robbed her blind. Took every dime she had. There's a warrant out for his arrest now, but that poor kid has got to be terrified."

"She's not really a kid," said Dom, trying to make sense of it all.

"She's a kid, Dom. The papers kept saying she was twenty-six, but she's not. She's just twenty-three. That's the other thing. They were forcing her to do adult scenes at just seventeen." Dom stopped at the door of the offices and looked at Zeke. "Seems to me this is the kind of thing we do. Just let Cam and Luke know if it's going to be you or one of the new boys." Dom nodded, watching as Zeke jogged up ahead, speaking with Luke, Cam, and Eric.

"Damn."

EXCERPT from DOM

The throngs of reporters and photographers outside the tiny apartment building were moving like vultures over their kill. The gate leading into the courtyard was closed securely by a keypad entry, but anyone with half a brain could figure it out or just wait until another resident entered.

Dom tried the number that Sly had given him for Leightyn once again, but it went straight to voicemail. Circling the block, he realized that the back of the building stretched against a four-story office building. Parking on the street, he jogged over and around to the back.

Pushing himself up onto a dumpster, he grabbed the fire escape ladder and walked up far enough to put himself even with the second-story balconies.

"Fuck, this is gonna hurt," he growled. With little room to move, he stepped back and launched himself toward the building. His body slammed into the iron balcony, hitting his midsection, causing him to gasp for air. "Fuck!"

He pulled himself over the side and bent forward, breathing deeply. Standing, he looked around the second-story U-shaped walkway and searched for Leightyn's apartment number. With a hand on his ribs, checking to be sure he hadn't broken them, he walked casually toward her door. Knocking soundly but not forcefully, he waited. Nothing. He knocked again.

"Leightyn? Leightyn, open up. It's me, Dom Quinn. Remember, Leightyn, I was your bodyguard while you were filming in New Orleans." He waited patiently, listening to see if there was any movement at all on the other side of the door. He knocked three more times.

"Leightyn? If you don't open the door, I'm gonna be forced to break it down, honey. I'm worried about you."

Just as he was about to shove a boot at the door, he heard the chain slide off, and the door was cracked just slightly, allowing him to see the big blue eyes of Leightyn.

"Hi," he smiled. "Rough day?"

"Rough year," she said, fighting back tears.

"Well, why don't you let me in, and we can talk about how to make it better?" he said, stepping back a bit so she could see that he was alone.

"I don't think anyone can make it better," she sniffed.

"I think I'm hurt by those remarks," he winked. "Let me try, Leightyn. Give me a chance, give my company a chance, and we'll at least make it better for you."

"Why? Why would you do this for me?" Dom rolled around the thoughts in his head. Why the fuck was he doing this? I mean, she was a pretty girl, but there were lots of pretty girls. Yes, their company did this sort of thing, but he could have sent anyone. He shook his head, knowing the answer.

"Let's just say it's in my DNA."

SERIES AND FAMILY GUIDE

(#) Book in Series	Name of Series	Character Name	Spouse	Child	Child's Spouse
1	*Reaper Security*	Joe "Nine" Dougall	Erin Richards	Joy Elizabeth "Ellie"	Jackson "Jax" Diaz
				Cameron	Kate Robicheaux
2	*Reaper Security*	Joseph "Trak" Redhawk	Lauren Owens	Sophia	Eric Bongard
				Suzette	Keith Robicheaux
				Nathan	Katrina Santos
				Joseph	Julia Anderson
3	*Reaper Security*	Billy Joe "Tailor" Bongard	Cholena "Lena" Blackwood	Eric	Sophia Ann Redhawk
4	*Reaper Security*	Dan "Wilson" Anderson	Sara MacMillan	Paige	Ryan Holden Robicheaux
				Julia	Joseph Redhawk
5	*Reaper Security*	Luke "Angel" Jordan	Mary Fitzhugh	Marc (Luke)	
				Georgianna	Carl Robicheaux
				Wesley	
6	*Reaper Security*	Peter "Miller" Robicheaux	Kari LeBlanc	Frank Gaspar	
7	*Reaper Security*	Rachelle Robicheaux	Frank "Mac" MacMillan	Danielle (Dani) Marie	Dev Parker
8	*Reaper Security*	Adele Robicheaux	Clay Duffy		
9	*Reaper Security*	Gabriel Robicheaux	Tory Gibson		
9	*Reaper Security*	John "Gibbie" Gibson	Dhara	Dalton	
9	*Reaper Security*	Antoine Robicheaux	Ella Stanton	Ryan Holden Robicheaux	Paige Anderson
9	*Reaper Security*	Gaspar Robicheaux	Alexandra Minsky	Luke	Ajei Blackwood
				Carl	Georgianna Jordan
				Ben	Harper Miller
				Adam	
	Steel Patriots			Violet	Striker Michaels
6	*Reaper Patriots*			Lucy	Alex "Sniff" Mullins
10	*Reaper Security*	William "Bull" Stone	Lily Bennett		
11	*Reaper Security*	Luc Robicheaux	Montana Divide		
12	*Reaper Security*	Raphael Robicheaux	Savannah O'Reilly	Ian Luke	Aspen Bodwick
				Katherine Gray "Kate"	Cameron Dougall
		Doug Graham	Deceased partner – Grip Current partner – Miguel Santos		
13	*Reaper Security*	Jasper "Jazz" Divide	Gray Vanzant	Virginia	Wes Jordan
14	*Reaper Security*	Baptiste Robicheaux	Rose Ellis	Elizabeth Irene "Liz"	Kiel Wolfkill
14	*Reaper Security*	Alec Robicheaux	Lissa Duncan	Keith	Susie Redhawk

(#) Book in Series	Name of Series	Character Name	Spouse	Child	Child's Spouse
15	Reaper Security	Stone Roberts	Bronwyn Ross		
16	Reaper Security	Suzette Robicheaux	Sylvester "Sly" DiMarco		
16	Reaper Security	Max Neill	Riley Corbett	CC	
17	Reaper Security	Titus Quinn	Olivia Baine	Lane	
				Dominic	
18	Reaper Security	Axel Doyle	Cait Brennan	Corey	
		Vince Martin	Ally Lawrence		
19	Reaper Security	Phoenix Keogh	Raven Foster		
	Reaper Security	Crow Foster			
19	Reaper Security	Wesley "Pigsty" O'Neal	Aasira "Sira" Al Aman		
20	Reaper Security	Zeke Wolfkill	Noelle Hart	Ezekiel ('Kiel)	Liz Divide
				Jane	Adam Robicheaux
20	Reaper Security	Elias Haggerty	Janie Granier		
20	Reaper Security	Russell "RJ" Jones	Celia Granier		
	Reaper Security	Chad Taylor			
	Reaper Security	Woody "Doc" Fine			
	Reaper Security	(d) Tony Parks			
	Reaper Security	(d) Alan Haley			
	Reaper Security	Michael Bodwick		Aspen	Ian Robicheaux
	Reaper Security	Miguel Santos	Doug	Katrina	Nathan Redhawk
	Reaper Security	Luke Robicheaux	Ajei Blackwood	Garrett	
1	My Seal Boys	Ian Shepard	Faith Gallagher	Kelsey Gallagher	Noa Lim
2	My Seal Boys	Noa Lim	Kelsey Gallagher		
3	My Seal Boys	Dave Carter	Ani Lim		
4	My Seal Boys	Lars Merrick	Jessica Fisher		
5	My Seal Boys	Trevor Banks	Ashley Dalton		
5	My Seal Boys	John Cruz	Camille Robicheaux		
6	My Seal Boys	Alec "Fitz" Fitzhenry	Zoe Myers		
7	My Seal Boys	Chris Paul	Elizabeth Broussard		
8	My Seal Boys	Luke O'Hara	Lucia Salvado		
8	My Seal Boys	Rory Baine	Piper Colley		
	My Seal Boys	(d) Anthony Garcia			
	My Seal Boys	Eric & Anna Tanner			
1	Steel Patriots MC	Eric "Ghost" Stanton	Grace Easton	(d) Faith & Hope	
				Jack Tyran "JT"	

(#) Book in Series	Name of Series	Character Name	Spouse	Child	Child's Spouse
				Eric Ryan	
2	*Steel Patriots MC*	Jack "Doc" Harris	Aubrey "Bree" Collins	Eva Irene	
3	*Steel Patriots MC*	Wade "Whiskey" English	Katrina Krevnyv	Juliette Rose	
4	*Steel Patriots MC*	Quincy "Zulu" Slater	Gabrielle London	Wade Eric	
				Tyler Gunner	
5	*Steel Patriots MC*	Gunner Michaels	Darby Greer	Calla	
6	*Steel Patriots MC*	Tyler "Tango" Green	Taylor Holland	Chase Maxwell	
7	*Steel Patriots MC*	Diego "Razor" Salcedo	Isabella "Bella" Castro		
8	*Steel Patriots MC*	Alex "Ace" Mills	Charlotte "CC" Robat" Tabor	Alexander John "AJ"	
9	*Steel Patriots MC*	Tyran "Eagle" O'Neal	Tinley Oakley	Tyran Eagle	
				Hawk Gunner	
				Benjamin Scott	
9	*Steel Patriots MC*	Ryan "Hawk" O'Neal	Keegan Oakley		
10	*Steel Patriots MC*	Scott "Skull" Crawford	Willa Ross (deceased)	Mathew Scott	
				Kevin Alexander	
11	*Steel Patriots MC*	Benjamin "Blade" LeBlanc	Suzette Doiron	Benjamin Alfonse	
12	*Steel Patriots MC*	Noah Anders	Tru Blanchard	William Rush	
13	*Steel Patriots MC*	Tristan Evers	Emma Colvin	Hannah Ivana	
14	*Steel Patriots MC*	Ivan Pechkin	Sophia Lord	William	
				Benjamin	
				Celeste	
				Cassidy	
				Carrie	
15	*Steel Patriots MC*	Griffin "Griff" James	Amanda Nettles		
16	*Steel Patriots MC*	Bryce Nolan	Ivy Brooks		
17	*Steel Patriots MC*	Kingston Miles	Claire Evers		
18	*Steel Patriots MC*	Grant Zimmerman	Everly "Evie" Johnson		
	Steel Patriots MC	Molly Walker	Asia	boy	
	Steel Patriots MC	George Robert Williamson	Mary		
	Steel Patriots MC	(d) Axel "Axe" Mains	(d) Decker "Ice" McManus		
	Steel Patriots MC	James Scarlutti			
	Steel Patriots MC	Chen Wu		Choi Wu	
	Steel Patriots MC	Ian Laughlin			
	Steel Patriots MC	Conor Laughlin			
	Steel Patriots MC	Vincent Scalia		(d) Isabella	

(#) Book in Series	Name of Series	Character Name	Spouse	Child	Child's Spouse
1	*Reaper-Patriots*	Dexter Lock	Marie Robicheaux		
2	*Reaper-Patriots*	Jean Robicheaux	Rose "Ro" Evers		
3	*Reaper-Patriots*	Jackson "Jax" Diaz	Joy "Ellie" Dougall		
4	*Reaper-Patriots*	Hunter Michaels	Megan Scott		
5	*Reaper-Patriots*	Carl Robicheaux	Penelope Georgianna "Georgie" Jordan		
6	*Reaper-Patriots*	Alex "Sniff" Mullins	Lucy Robicheaux	Caroline Willa	
7	*Reaper-Patriots*	Cameron "Cam" Dougall	Kate Robicheaux	Ian William	
8	*Reaper-Patriots*	Keith Robicheaux	Suzette "Susie" Redhawk	Joseph Alec Keith (JAK)	
9	*Reaper-Patriots*	Eric Bongard	Sophia Ann Redhawk	Billy Joseph	
10	*Reaper-Patriots*	Joseph Redhawk	Julia Anderson	Joseph Billy (JB)	
				Tobias Franklin	
11	*Reaper-Patriots*	Ryan Robicheaux (Holden)	Paige Anderson	Dan Antoine	
12	*Reaper-Patriots*	Nathan Redhawk	Katrina Santos	Nathan Luke	
				Michael Douglas	
13	*Reaper-Patriots*	Ben Robicheaux	Harper Miller		
14	*Reaper-Patriots*	Sean Liffey	Shay Miller		
15	*Reaper-Patriots*	Ezekiel 'Kiel' Wolfkill	Elizabeth 'Liz' Robicheaux	Everett Baptiste	
				Eastman Matthew	
				Ethan Ezekiel	
16	*Reaper-Patriots*	Ian Robicheaux	Aspen Bodwick		
17	*Reaper-Patriots*	Adam Robicheaux	Jane Wolfkill		
18	*Reaper-Patriots*	Marc Jordan	Ela Wolfkill		
19	*Reaper-Patriots*	Wes Jordan	Virginia Divide	(preg)	
20	*Reaper-Patriots*	Aiden Wagner	Brit Elig		
21	*Reaper-Patriots*	Devin Parker	Danielle 'Dani' MacMillan		
22	*Reaper-Patriots*	Dalton Gibson	Calla Michaels		
23	*Reaper-Patriots*	Frank Robicheaux	Lane Quinn		

OTHER BOOKS BY MARY KENNEDY YOU MIGHT ENJOY!

REAPER Security Series
Erin's' Hero
Lauren's Warrior
Lena's' Mountain
Sara's' Chance
Mary's Angel
Kari's Gargoyle
Rachelle's Savior
Adele's Heart
Tori's' Secret
Finding Lily
Montana Rules
Savannah Rain
Gray Skies
My First Choice
Three Wishes
Second Chances
One Day at a Time
When You Least Expect It
Missing Hearts
Trail of Love

My SEAL Boys (connections to the REAPER Series)
Ian
Noa
Carter
Lars
Trevor
Fitz
Chris
O'Hara

Steel Patriots MC Series
Ghost – Book One
Doc – Book Two
Whiskey – Book Three
Zulu – Book Four
Gunner – Book Five
Tango – Book Six
Razor – Book Seven
Ace – Book Eight
Hawk & Eagle – Book Nine
Skull – Book Ten
Blade – Book Eleven
Noah – Book Twelve
Tristan – Book Thirteen
Ivan – Book Fourteen
Griff – Book Fifteen

Steel Patriots MC Series (continued)
Bryce – Book Sixteen
King – Book Seventeen
Grant – Book Eighteen
Striker – Book Nineteen

REAPER-Patriots Series
Dex – Book One
Jean – Book Two
Jax – Book Three
Hunter – Book Four
Carl – Book Five
Sniff – Book Six
Cam – Book Seven
Keith – Book Eight
Eric – Book Nine
Joseph – Book Ten
Ryan – Book Eleven
Nathan – Book Twelve
Ben – Book Thirteen
Sean – Book Fourteen
Kiel – Book Fifteen
Ian – Book Sixteen
Adam – Book Seventeen
Marc – Book Eighteen
Wes – Book Nineteen
Aiden – Book Twenty
Parker – Book Twenty-one
Dalton – Book Twenty-two
Frank – Book Twenty-three

REAPER-Patriots Christmas: Do You Believe?

Strange Gifts Series
Dark Visions
Dark Medicine
Dark Flame

ABOUT THE AUTHOR

Mary Kennedy is the mother of two adult children, has an amazing son-in-law, and is grandmother to two beautiful grandsons. She works full-time at a job she loves, and writing is her creative outlet. She lives in Texas and enjoys traveling, reading, and cooking. Her passion for assisting veterans and veteran causes comes from a strong military family background. Mary loves to hear from her readers and encourages them to join her mailing list, as she'll keep you up-to-date on new releases at https://insatiableink.squarespace.com. You can also join her Facebook page at Insatiable Ink.

Dear Readers,

I love hearing from you and encourage you to visit my website insatiableink.squarespace.com. Let me know your thoughts and ideas on new books or expanding on characters. It's also a safe space to give your own feelings, like those of the characters. I love reading about how you relate to the stories because as we all know, there's a little of each of them within us.

I look forward to hearing from you and hope you enjoy other books in my collections.

Explore… and enjoy!

Printed in Great Britain
by Amazon